THE
Love Mosaic

Edited by *Dr. C. White-Elliott*

This book contains works of both non-fiction and fiction. In the cases of fictional writings, the stories may have been fashioned after true stories but are not exact retellings.

CLF Publishing, LLC.
9161 Sierra Ave, Ste. 203C
Fontana, CA 92335
www.clfpublishing.org

ISBN # 978-0-9961971-0-6

Printed in the United States of America.

Dedications

This book is dedicated to all aspiring writers who were told they couldn't make it in the field of writing or who may have been too scared to move forward because of a fear of failure.

The seventeen authors, whose stories are included within, are proof that you can be successful and your dreams can be a reality.

So, I invite you to pursue your own writing and be the success you know you are.

C. White-Elliott

Dr. Cassundra White-Elliott

Acknowledgements

I acknowledge all the participants in this project, who helped to see it from its stages of inception to its complete fruition.

May your success be plentiful, as you continue to pursue your educational and writing endeavors. I look forward to working with each of you individually, collectively, or both, in the near future.

Much love and appreciation,

C. White-Elliott

Dr. Cassundra White-Elliott

Table of Contents

Introduction

Welcome to *The Love Mosaic*, where you will enter the exciting world of short stories, which all revolve around the topic of love. Here, the imagination can and will unfold right before your very eyes. What you least expect just may become the expected.

The seventeen authors have delved within their own imaginations and pulled out all the stops and barred no holds. Their tales will excite you, cause curiosity to grow, bring tears of sadness, and/or even feelings of wonderment.

They are skillful in their craft, and they are to be congratulated for their efforts. Some have stepped into unknown territory with publishing and sharing their talents with the world at large.

So, I invite you to sit back, relax with your favorite drink, curl up in your most comfortable chair and be prepared for the journeys that lie ahead.

With no further ado, I invite you to ENJOY!!!!!!!!!!!

Love

Elizabeth Barrett Browning, 1806 – 1861

We cannot live, except thus mutually
We alternate, aware or unaware,
The reflex act of life: and when we bear
Our virtue onward most impulsively,
Most full of invocation, and to be
Most instantly compellant, certes, there
We live most life, whoever breathes most air
And counts his dying years by sun and sea.
But when a soul, by choice and conscience, doth
Throw out her full force on another soul,
The conscience and the concentration both make
mere life, Love. For Life in perfect whole
And aim consummated, is Love in sooth,
As nature's magnet-heat rounds pole with pole.

Extraordinary Love

Katie Abbott

"There could have been no two hearts so open,

no tastes so similar,

no feelings so in unison."

Jane Austen – *Persuasion*

On October 30, 1986, something seemingly normal happened. Most people would consider it to be normal, but it is in fact something extraordinary. Two very special people met that night. They thought it was just going to be a casual double date with their mutual friends, but it turned into so much more; something that would start a 27-year journey.

Brooke was a seemingly normal girl. You would never know by looking at her that she had a nightmare of a childhood. She never let herself get down about it. She knew there was a plan for her life, and it was even more amazing than she could have possibly imagined. She was just a normal college girl to everyone else. She worked in the school library because of her love for reading and being around books. She wasn't a party girl, but she also wasn't a hermit. She was the perfect college student. But whenever she would go out on a date, there was always missing something. She was never able to feel that connection that everyone seems to be searching for.

Mike was a normal guy. He was on his way to becoming an engineer. He had always loved cars and sports. Other than his friends and family, those were his two loves. As a UCLA alumnus, he was very passionate about anything Bruins. He was born and raised in Southern California, so that automatically made him loyal to the Los Angeles Lakers. He had always been that guy that everyone liked and wanted to be friends with. He was the popular guy in high school who played sports and was senior class president. He grew up in a house with his mom and two grandparents. Mike's grandfather taught him everything he knew about cars. Mike could take a car apart and put it back together. But, like Brooke, he was missing that feeling and connection with someone.

One weekend, Mike was planning on visiting a childhood friend who was going to school in San Diego. Mike was just expecting a casual weekend over Halloween. It turned out that his friend, who was also named Mike, wanted to spend the weekend with his girlfriend, but reassured him that his girlfriend had a cousin who was single. Mike agreed to still go down, and he was actually excited to meet this girl. So, Mike drove down with Kristin, his friend's girlfriend; the entire time, she talked about her cousin Brooke. Brooke was working her sorority's Halloween booth at the school Halloween event, when they arrived in San Diego. Kristin rushed down the hill from the parking lot toward the event. Mike was looking down at Kristin to see where she was going. Right as he was about to walk down the hill, someone he knew called after him to chat. Right at that moment, Kristin was pointing him out to Brooke. All Brooke could see from there was his dark brown curly hair. When Mike made it to the booth, he saw Brooke for the first time. She was in a magician costume for her booth. He was mesmerized by her. She was dressed in nice black pants and a crisp white button-down shirt. She had put silver sparkles all over her face, and Mike could hardly stop staring at her big, beautiful hazel eyes and her long brown hair.

After Mike met up with his friend and Brooke cleaned up her booth after the event, they all met up and headed out. They decided to go to a small Mexican restaurant that made the best rolled tacos. The entire time, Mike could hardly take his eyes off Brooke. She was the most beautiful woman he had ever seen. They both never wanted the date to end, even though they knew they were going to see each other the next day. They talked the entire time and couldn't imagine a better first date.

The next day, the two couples just hung out on campus since Kristin was staying with Brooke, and Mike was staying with the other Mike. On Sunday, they all got up and went to church and then walked around Seaport Village. They hung out all day, and when it came to the time Mike and Kristin had to leave to go back home, no one wanted to go.

Brooke didn't want the weekend to end, and Mike didn't want to leave, but they knew that wasn't going to be the end. They were pretty much official already, so there was no point in trying to avoid it. Once Mike and Kristin left, everyone was sad that the best weekend ever had to end. But the real surprise came the next day. Brooke was in her dorm on Monday, and she got a call from the front desk telling her she had a delivery. She went up the stairs and saw she had received a huge flower arrangement. She knew exactly who they were from before she read the card. Mike had sent her the biggest bunch of flowers Brooke had ever seen. She beamed with pride as she walked down the corridor of her floor as everyone saw her flowers.

Over the next few months, Mike and Brooke would talk on the phone every day for at least three hours.

They talked about everything; nothing was off limits. They both wanted to know everything about one another, even the stuff that wasn't always flattering. Their love for each other grew fast, but true. Because Mike lived in Buena Park, about three hours away, they talked on the phone more than anything else. They would travel back and forth most weekends, and when the semester was over, Brooke had to travel back to Texas where her parents were. She didn't want to be that far away from Mike for that long, but it was only a month.

During that time, Mike knew Brooke was the person he wanted to spend his life with. So, he picked out a ring and had a whole plan for when he was going to propose. He had even called her dad and asked for his permission. Even though Mike was only 23 and Brooke was 20, he just knew there wasn't anyone in the entire world that could make him feel the way he felt about her.

Brooke had been back in school for a few weeks and knew Mike was planning something, but she didn't know what or when. She was just waiting in anticipation. One weekend, Mike was planning on visiting her, but she had to do a fundraiser for her sorority and had to cancel.

Later that night, Mike called Brooke's dorm room and her roommate answered. Mike asked where Brooke was, and her roommate said she wasn't there. He asked if the fundraiser was over yet, and she told him that it was cancelled. After he hung up the phone, he figured out that she was going to surprise him, but he wouldn't let her. He told his family his plan for the night. He grabbed the little black box from his nightstand and rushed to the train station. Her train came in earlier than what he had expected. He wanted to propose while she was still on the train platform. But by the time he got to her, she was already off the platform, and he didn't want to make her get back on the platform. Brooke was so excited because she thought she had finally surprised him, but when she stepped off the train, there he was walking towards her. *Of course he is there, he knows everything*, she thought.

He took her to his car, and he was trying to formulate a new plan. She knew the route he usually took to his house, so she would question why he was taking a different route. The entire ride home he was trying to figure out a new plan. He had to do it that night because he had already told his family his plan.

He pulled into the driveway, and before she could get out of the car, he pulled her aside and asked her, "What would you say of I asked you to marry me?" Brooke chuckled and said jokingly, "Show me a ring, and I'll tell you." Then, Mike pulled out the little black box and opened it and simply asked, "Will you marry me?" Brooke was stunned, not expecting for him to actually propose. She simply looked up at him and said, "Yes." She loved Mike more than anything, and Mike knew she was the one after their first weekend together.

Six months later on July 30, 1987, Mike and Brooke were married in front of all of their friends and family. Kristin was Brooke's maid of honor and Mike's friend Mike was his best man. Mike and Brooke may not have been the perfect couple, but they were perfect for each other, and no one ever doubted their relationship. Everyone could tell how much they loved each other. Both of them had gone through so much and even through all of that, they loved each other and knew that whatever came their way, they could make it through because they believed in each other. They didn't care what baggage the other was carrying because it didn't matter; all that mattered was each other.

Now almost 27 years and 3 kids later, they are even more in love now than they were they day they got married.

About the Author

Katie Abbott is twenty years old. She was born and raised in Southern California. She has two wonderful parents and two brothers. She has always loved reading, but she was never interested in writing only until recently. So, her goals have recently changed. She desired to major in psychology, but she recently decided to major in English and pursue a career in editing. Getting to read something new every day and to examine other's imagination and format it into something beautiful sounds like something she could do forever.

Unrequited

"Lone Heart"

Samantha Blackwell

The pale rosy glow
Of winter's cruel cold
Elegantly paints your skin.

Though I stand by
Heart in my throat, at the sight
My eyes proceed to roam.

Too entranced to leave,
Too embarrassed to stare.
My hands, ah! How they tremble.
Is it discernable? Aye, I fear it so,
My girlish blush betrays me.

My knees turn to butter
My thighs do quake,
I fear they can't hold my weight.

With sentence half finished.
Heart too full, my hunger unyielding
I turn away.

Though my body does exit
your exquisite presence
my heart and my mind remain.

With sighs un-uttered,
And desires un-gained
I let my lone heart

Erode away.

Picture and Poem by Samantha Blackwell

I

Princess Alexandra looked out upon the battlefield with deep, brooding eyes. She wondered, not for the first time, if the forfeiting of so many lives over who should wear the crown would be worth it in the end.

As the dying warriors were taken off the battlefield to the healers, Alexandra marveled at the short memories of all people, how they had so quickly disregarded the honored Final Will of King Mathew, her father. He had wished Alexandra, his eldest child, to rule once his life had expired. After the king's death, there was a split of wills between the politicians. Some wished the Final Will of the king to be carried out; others said Princess Alexandra's younger brother Prince Andrew would be a more appropriate ruler. Prince Andrew had then refused the crown saying that he wished his sister to rule just as their father had wished.

However, after Prince Andrew's declaration, another male candidate was found to be crowned: Alexandra's older cousin, Duke Rupert. The argument in Rupert's favor for kingship was a flimsy one, and it became obvious to everyone the politicians supporting the duke's succession were driven by the ignorant prejudice that a woman had no place in politics.

From then on, the council was split into two factions. Those members of parliament who supported Duke Rupert's succession were tactfully referred to as "Rebels" because calling them traitors at that delicate point in time would have started a war, which was the last thing anyone had wanted. The other party was referred to as the Radicals; these were the councilmen that defended Alexandra's legacy.

Not too long after the split, Alexandra's life was threatened and an assassination was attempted to be carried out, though it was found out and stopped. Those who could be proven guilty were imprisoned, and some were executed.

****

Alexandra continued to gaze upon the battlefield as the memories flooded her mind. She looked at the bodies of friends and foes, all countrymen who had left their homes and families, for what they thought was right. She turned her horse around and began to make her way back toward camp; her two armed escorts did the same.

The rising sun was red, making the blood soaked ground look jet black. The princess felt guilty that she did not help her troops on the battlefield, but even though Alexandra knew how to fight, it was still unthinkable for her councilors to allow her to be in combat.

As they neared camp, it grew impossible for the horses not to tread on some of the bodies. Alexandra would have preferred to walk on foot, but Captain Samuel would not have tolerated it even if his guards allowed it. She sighed as she reflected on how much everything had changed because she had been born a girl and not a boy. Maybe if she had married things would have been better, maybe not. When a war seemed inevitable, the Rebels had hinted that some would consider switching sides, if Alexandra would marry. The princess was somewhat disturbed by this, for her mother had taught her to marry for love, not power. After all, had not her father, the king, not broken tradition to marry Alexandra's mother, a commoner?

Despite her reluctance, the Radicals sent emissaries to other countries seeking a fit marriage; none were successful. In a cruel twist of fate, there were few unmarried noblemen within the kingdom of Othos, with the exception of Alexandra's cousin Rupert, whom Alexandra would not consider, for what seemed to her obvious reasons. However, there were those on the Rebel's side and on the Radical's side who argued that one woman marrying her first cousin was a low price to pay to avoid bloodshed.

Outraged, Princess Alexandra declared in parliament that though she was only one woman, she would be queen, and she refused to take part in a nuptial agreement that would make a tavern wench ashamed. Duke Rupert was present at the meeting and took offence. That night, the second assassin was sent to Alexandra's bed chamber but was caught by a guard. The assassin, under torture, named Rupert as his employer. However, without the original documents, the Rebels claimed that the assassin was a liar. Rupert soon thereafter left the castle and gathered an army, and so the war began.

****

Alexandra and her escorts dismounted their steeds as soon as they reached the edge of camp. After handing the horses over to their caretakers, the trio began to make their way towards the conference tent. Along the way, Alexandra insisted upon making frequent stops to greet her soldiers.

Many had advised Alexandra against coming to the final battles, but she refused to consider another course; her loyal subjects were fighting and dying for her birthright. In her mind, it would be disrespectful to the warriors and their families if she was not present during the last battles. There was no doubt that the war was coming to an end. Rupert's forces had suffered many losses and had been forced to fall back into their last fortress, where it had been held under siege ever since.

That morning's battle was caused when the Rebels had attempted to catch the Radicals off guard, in hopes of capturing or killing Princess Alexandra or Prince Andrew. However, the ambush had been spotted by the Radical's watchmen, so they were ready long before the ambush had arrived and the fighting ended before the sun had cleared the horizon. The only way the Rebels could have known that the royals were there was the possibility of a spy. Who it was the Radicals did not know, which was why they had called a meeting in the conference tent.

****

When Alexandra was within sight of the conference tent, there was a strange absenteeism of soldiers. Besides the sound of the wind making the canvas sides of the tents ripple, there was complete silence. It was as if a god had placed a bubble to encompass the area surrounding Alexandra and her guards, which blocked out all sounds of life.

Uneasy, her guards drew their swords and stepped in front of her before they cautiously continued making their way toward the tent. They were halfway there when all three of them clearly heard the click of a trigger, followed instantly by the twang of a spring and the noise of something small whizzing through the air towards them.

The poisonous dart hit one of Alexandra's guards in the side of the neck. The guard reached up impulsively and pulled the dart out of him, but it was too late. He staggered and fell as the poison was pumped into his brain along with his blood.

The other guard grabbed Alexandra and pulled her down to the ground.

"Keep your head low, your highness," he ordered just as his companion's eyes rolled back into his head. His face was contorted with pain, and after a convulsion, he moved no more.

At that same moment, there was another twang of a spring, and the second guard was hit in the eye with another dart.

"May the gods preserve this true queen of Othos," the man cried just before he died.

The conference tent entrance flap burst open, just as the shout of the soldier began to die and the Radical commanders, who had gathered within the conference tent, spilled out. At the same time, other tents were being emptied of their occupants; only they weren't wearing the colors of the Radicals, but that of the Rebels.

The Rebels intercepted the commanders from reaching Alexandra, and a fight ensued. A lone Rebel soldier turned tail and started making his way towards the princess. She scrambled to her feet and drew her slender scabbard from its sheath.

The Rebel was mere feet away from engaging her when suddenly he fell to his knees, a dart protruding from his left temple; it took a mere second for him to die.

The princess looked in the direction that the dart had come from and saw a neat square hole cut into the side of a tent about five feet away from her. It took a moment for her to realize that there was a pair of gray eyes looking back at her through the hole. Right below the eyes was the tip of a dart thrower.

Sheathing her sword, Alexandra turned and ran; the kingdom wouldn't be any good with a dead sovereign. Dodging behind several tents and out of sight of the dart thrower, she continued to run. She wasn't shocked to discover that there wasn't a single Radical soldier anywhere. Most of her forces were either collecting the wounded and dead or going to the food tents for their morning rations. The nearest meal tent was in the opposite direction of where she had been forced to flee due to the position of the dart thrower. She also didn't know how many of her men were killed when the Rebels had invaded her camp.

As she ran towards the sanctuary of the woods, not daring to hide in any of the tents in case they were occupied by Rebels, it became clear to the princess that the early morning ambush had been meant to distract the Radicals, while a smaller Rebel force

30

invaded the opposite end of the camp from the woods. When all of the leaders of the Radicals were assembled in the conference tent, they would have the Radicals in their power. If Alexandra's guards had not noticed something was wrong before entering the conference tent, the war would have ended in the Rebel's favor. It seemed more likely to her now that there was a traitor of high rank present in the Radical army, rather than a spy. Alexandra knew the best thing for her to do would be to hide in the woods until she could formulate a plan on how she should smoke out the traitor.

She had cleared all of the tents and was within sight of the woods when she saw in her peripheral vision someone draped in a black cloak running on foot out from behind some of the tents farther down the camp. The princess didn't slow her pace to see who it was, but she began to run in zigzags to avoid becoming victim to an arrow or a dart. Stones clattered beneath her feet as she neared the bank of the river, which was a hundred yards from the entrance of the woods.

Her breath was becoming labored, and her legs burned from the exertion. She was about to enter the shallow water when the runner she had seen exit the camp skidded in front of her, a mini wave of water flew about their feet as they stopped.

The princess dug her heels into the bank to stop her run. Her boots went beneath the rocks and skidded across the wet sand beneath them. She came to a halt a couple of yards away from the stranger.

"You runnest like the frightened rabbit before the fox m'lady."

Alexandra started when she realized that the stranger before her was a woman. Her appearance was extremely rough with strong features like that of a man with two emotionless grey eyes staring out of a deeply tanned leathery-looking face.

"I see the fox is swifter this time, even though the hare had a fair start," Alexandra panted.

"Aye," the stranger said, a smirk threatening to cover her lips as she lifted up a small dart thrower. "I don't get paid if someone else kills my target for me, ye know." The woman tilted her head, as she examined her victim. "I know you're a great lady. I've been followin' your struggles with no small interest in the tavern gossip. I gain no great pleasure in murderin' your highness. Do you forgive me for brin' about your death, for this is the only way I can earn a livin'.'"

Alexandra looked into the woman's unfeeling eyes. She didn't bother to draw her sword. It was useless against a dart thrower, and there was no point in trying to run again.

"No," Alexandra replied. "I can't forgive you for leaving my people in turmoil and without their true sovereign to lead them in this war. I do not forgive you for working for my greatest enemy and the enemy of my people: my cousin Rupert, who is darkness of ignorance itself. Working for him makes you dark also."

"I can forgive you for taking my life, as a life of one woman, but I cannot forgive you for all you take from my people." She spoke strongly and with passion, keeping her head high and her eyes on those of her third and final assassin.

The strange woman was the first to break their locked gaze as she lifted her dart thrower.

"I wish you had hired me first," she said. "Be that as it may, you're too honorable for such a deed." She took aim.

"May I make a request? Not as a prince but as a woman?"

"What is it m'lady?" the mercenary lowered her dart thrower a fraction of an inch.

"You appear to me as a woman who can get in and out of places unseen. Would you take care to deliver this to Captain Samuel?" Alexandra pulled a small slip of parchment out of a secret pouch on her belt. "I carry this with me every waking hour, in case it is my last. I am afraid that my brother or a member of my council shall destroy it, to save my honor. However, it is of the greatest importance that it be delivered."

"It shall be done with great pride, m'lady."

"A thousand times thank you," Alexandra sighed with relief as she heard the dart thrower spring sound for the last time.

II

After Captain Samuel cut down the last Rebel soldier, he looked around. Some of the other Radical commanders were wounded. A small amount of relief rushed through him as he realized none were killed.

The captain raised his voice and asked who could still run. Six gave an affirmative. One he sent to find a healer, two he ordered to stay with the wounded, and the remaining final three he ordered to come with him in search of the princess. Prince Andrew wanted to come with them, but Captain Samuel ordered him to stay. Besides, the prince appeared to have several broken ribs.

It took the captain and the other three commanders very little time to find the princess's trail and follow it to her body with a dart still in her jugular. Death must have come quickly. She looked more peaceful and happier to Samuel than he had seen her since her father had died.

One of Alexandra's oldest advisors, who was one of the search party, howled like a wounded animal as he fell to his knees and wept like a small child. The sight sent the other two men on the brink of tears, but not the captain. "Pull yourselves together," he snapped over the noise.

"Show the man some pity, sir! The girl was like a daughter to him," one of the others retorted.

"I wasn't speaking to him," Samuel replied. "One of you stay with him. The other will come with me once you feel like gaining some of your manhood back."

The two commanders straightened automatically but did not comment. One stepped forward.

Samuel thought that was as good as volunteering to go. Turning on his heel, he began searching for signs of where the killer of the princess had gone. Once he had found the assassin's wet footprints on the stones exiting the river, they began tracking. Before long, the pair found themselves near the captain's own tent.

"Do you think it's a coincidence?" Samuel asked aloud.

"There are no coincidences when you're dealing with hired killers," his companion replied.

"You sound as if you speak from experience."

His companion was silent. Samuel decided not to press him. The man was a lord of whom Samuel knew little about, and the captain really didn't care to know. All the lords were the same money-grubbing mongrels, as far as he could tell. The cost of food and horses had risen enormously due to the war, and many a lord who had the resources stood to make a large profit, while their poorer countrymen starved for want of money to buy the food. Samuel didn't need to know who this lord had needed to have murdered in order to make his pocketbook fatter; he just wanted information. "Well, I've never dealt with an assassin. What do you advise we do?" the captain asked halting around the corner from his tent. Upon reflection, he found the man's statement rather odd; they had no way of knowing for sure if the killer of the princess was hired, but he decided that then was not the time to ask.

"I say we go on ahead," the other replied. "If the killer is after your head, he won't give up until he has it. Better to and try and kill him while we know where he is; worse comes to worse, you'll die on your feet."

Samuel agreed, and the two planned to split up: the captain going in the front, while the other circled around to the back.

****

The assassin had just placed the note on Samuel's pillow and was about to leave when she saw the captain coming towards the tent. He hadn't noticed her; she fled to the rear of the tent and exited. As soon as she had, she found herself facing a man dressed in the Radical colors.

She didn't have time to load her dart thrower before he was bearing down upon her. Dodging the heavy sword, she drew out a knife and stabbed him between the ribs.

He howled as she yanked the knife out and began to run.

"Coward," the commander cried. "Coward!"

The assassin turned on her heels and threw the knife at the man's face before he could cry out the hated word again.

"Coward is better than traitor," she spat on the dead man's body.

That's when the captain burst through the tent's back entrance, sword drawn.

"I have no fight with you," the assassin said calmly.

"I think we do. You are the murderer of my rightful sovereign. Let me hear you deny it."

"I can't deny the truth," she replied coolly.

"Then, I cannot let you leave, but before we begin, I want you to explain your statement to him," Samuel demanded while gesturing towards the body of the man she had just killed, without looking away from her.

"He was the traitor that told the Rebels that the royalty were here," the woman explained. "Only D'ke Rupert and I knew about 'im. He ne'er liked my knowin' 'bout 'im." As she spoke she unstrapped her dart gun from her shoulder and placed it on the

38

ground. Stepping forward, she drew a thin sword from the sheath on her back. She made the first move, and the duel began. Before a minute had passed, he knocked the sword out of her hand. Quickly pulling out another knife, she cut his wrist. As he switched hands, she had time to stab him in the leg. She had no wish to kill him, just handicap him, so she could have a chance to get away, but before she could drawback, he cut her hand off. Letting out a brief scream, she turned and dived for her dart thrower. The assassin was close to tears as she dropped the thrower and dart, unable to reload with one hand.

The captain laid his injured hand on her shoulder, his other hand still held his sword.

"It's time to yield," he said; he's teeth clenched from pain.

The woman would not look up into his face. Slowly, she nodded and stood defeated. She allowed him to lead her to the army prison.

III

Samuel trudged back to his tent. It was now late in the evening, and he needed to rest. So much had happened…

After the assassin had made a written confession (despite her rather poor grammar, she had superb handwriting), she provided an assassination contract between herself and Rupert for the death of the princess with Rupert's signature and seal. Once these documents were locked away safely, they did the same with the assassin.

Samuel and the other commanders had gathered to discuss what was to be done next. They spoke with Prince Andrew, who was now by rights the legitimate heir to the throne. He said they should continue the siege until Duke Rupert was handed over for organizing the murder of Princess Alexandra. He did not expect any of the Rebels to stick with Rupert since now his sister was dead. The Radical commanders agreed and sent messengers to the fortress conveying the demand.

Before the sun set, the duke was handed over by the Rebels, who were joyously proclaiming their loyalty to Andrew. Now that Duke Rupert was under lock and key, the Radical army was paid and allowed to disembark for their homes.

The camp was a sight of mourning. All had been looking forward to the end of the war, but they had always assumed that Alexandra would be with them when it happened. The entire war was a failure: Othos would not have the Queen that they had fought so long and hard to gain.

Captain Samuel sat down wearily on his cot. He could not find tears to shed for his Alexandra. She had been his princess, leader, councilor and friend. She had been his hope, faith and love: such a loss couldn't be remedied by tears.

Samuel swung his legs onto his cot and laid his head on a piece of parchment, which was lying on top of his pillow. He sat back up again and looked at it. Using the dim light of the dying sun coming through the opening in his tent, he saw it was a note addressed to him in Alexandra's familiar handwriting. He sat and stared at it for a moment, wondering how it could have gotten there. There was only one possibility. The captain slipped the note into his pocket before leaving to visit the army lockup.

The assassin was chained to a stake that was imbedded in the ground at the center of the army prison tent. After Samuel asked the prison guard to leave, she looked up at him with those disinterested grey eyes.

"Why were you in my tent?" When she didn't answer, he prodded, "Were you there to deliver something?"

"If you're knowin' the answer, why put out the question?"

"I just want to know the truth," he replied.

"There's no truth," the disheartened woman said, "just what you acce'."

"So, if you chose to not accept that you lost a hand, would you get it back?" Samuel snapped, "If you didn't accept you are in prison and aren't getting out, it would no longer be so?"

"It ain't so," she was suddenly on her feet. The chain that bound her fell to the ground with broken links. She kneed Samuel in the stomach, and he fell to the ground spluttering. Using her remaining hand, she pulled out his sword and pointed the tip at his heart.

"I will not be ke' in prison; I will not lose my hand," she hissed. "You hear good boy; a woman who was as good a dead wished that le'er be read by you, and I did make it so. You can acce', or don't, but it ends." The assassin slashed the captain's cheek with the sword. While he was distracted with the pain, she pulled a tiny vile out of a hidden compartment in the heel of her boot. The assassin downed the contents in the vile in one gulp. Before the captain could get back to his feet, she had lost her balance and toppled over. The captain called out for help, but she couldn't be saved.

Once Samuel and the guard decided not to inform the other commanders until morning about the demise of the assassin, Samuel re-entered the privacy of his tent, after a brief visit to the healers to get his slashed cheek sewn together. Then, he finally read the note.

> *I will wait for you outside the gates of the afterlife.*

The phrase hit Samuel like an iron fist, and his mind was lost in a sea of memories:

Waiting, yes that's what Alexandra and Samuel had done from the beginning.

After they had made vows to each other as children, they needed to wait for Samuel to make the slow climb from stable boy to knight.

Then, when it was suggested that she marry one of a higher rank than knight, the two became afraid they would never be together.

When the danger of an unwanted marriage was over, the war had started.

No matter how long they waited, they always needed to wait some more.

Captain Samuel would put off seeing his beloved, so he could help his country and countryman, until Death took his life.

Princess Alexandra would not move on to see her deceased family until her knight joined her.

Through their lives, they had been separated by rank, duty, greed, honor and war, but nothing would stop them from making their final adventure together.

About the Author

Samantha Blackwell is an artist in the broadest sense of the word: writer, tactile artist, poet, pianist, actress and playwright. She has her fingers in a lot of pies. Her first published work was a self-published children's book entitled "My Magical World." Since its original publication in 2011, she has self-published two anthologies "A Slice of Life: Death" and "Samantha's Animal Tales." All of her projects and social media outlets can be found at www.samanthablackwell.xyz.

DON'T TEXT & CRY

Michael Bril

"Anyone can fall in love.

They just have to let their guard down."

Michael Bril

Joanna sat on the park bench looking motionless at the text she just received. Her eyes began to sting. She stuffed the phone back into her pocket as her vision blurred. She leaned forward to stare at the ground. A single teardrop rolled past her eyelid and splattered on the pavement.

She was supposed to meet her boyfriend for a lovely Sunday afternoon at the park, but instead he decided to humiliate her with a break-up text. She was shattered- to say the least. In person would have been better. Heck, even a call would have been more humane! But no, those pixilated words rang in Joanna's mind, as she got lost in her emotions.

A few minutes later, she forced herself to stop. She tried to dry her tears with her sleeve, but her face still felt like a snotty mess. She wanted to turn away from anyone who might see her like that.

Eventually, she pulled herself together. She looked around the park. Warm rays of sun graced the day. Clouds scattered across the sky, making patches of shade across the grass. Kids jumped up and down on the seesaw, parents sizzled hotdogs and ribs on their grills, and lovers rolled in the grass whispering secrets into each other's ears.

She brought her feet up on the bench and rested her head on her knees, occasionally sniffing involuntarily. After taking a deep breath, she closed her eyes.

"Why are you sad?" a voice startled her. She looked to see a small boy wearing blue overalls.

Wiping her eyes again, she asked, "What makes you think I'm sad?"

"I saw you crying, and I came to give you this." He handed Joanna a yellow dandelion. "It will make you feel better. I'm Ricky. What's your name?"

Joanna glanced at the dandelion, then at Ricky. She didn't much change her tone for the boy. "Thanks," she said. "I'm Joanna."

"Nice to meet you, Joanna." Ricky leapt next to her on the bench. "So, why are you sad, Joanna?"

"Oh," she hesitated, "it's grown up stuff."

"That's okay, you can tell me," Ricky said kicking his dangling feet around. "Mommy said I'm mature for my age."

Joanna raised an eyebrow. "Is that so?"

Ricky nodded enthusiastically.

"Well, if you insist," she said. "You see... My boyfriend broke up with me."

"What!" Ricky grabbed his hair in exaggerated

shock. "Why'd he do that?"

Joanna shook her head. "I don't know."

"He's stupid," Ricky laughed.

"Stupid?" Joanna found herself giggling along.

"Yeah," he said. "He's silly because you're too pretty to broke."

She curled her cheeks into a smile. "Don't say that. Looks aren't everything you know. You need to be able to talk with each other and trust each other."

"All that?" Ricky said, rubbing his scalp.

"Yes, and more," Joanna said. "You also need to be happy with one another."

"Hmm," Ricky scratched his chin. "Were you happy?"

Joanna gave it some thought, "Yeah, I suppose we were happy."

"Did you guys talk good?"

"Well… we argued a little."

Ricky began to play with his thumbs. "That's okay, my mommy and daddy argue too. Mommy says that you argue with the people you love, and that's a way to tell that you love them."

"I'm not sure it works like that all the time," Joanna said. "Where are your parents anyway?"

"My mommy's by the playground. Don't worry. I'm not lost."

Joanna stared at the playground full of children. For a moment, she spaced out.

"Well, did you love him?" Ricky brought her back.

"Who?"

"Your boyfriend, silly." He poked her shoulder.

"Oh," she paused. "I don't know."

"Then, why were you sad?"

Joanna went over her memories of her relationship. "Maybe I was overreacting," she said. "Sometimes kids cry over candy. I guess this is like the same thing." She put the dandelion to her nose. It smelled like rain.

"Those are supposed to be good for you my teacher says," said Ricky.

"Thanks for that."

"Don't worry; I'm sure you will find a boyfriend who makes you happy." Without thinking, Ricky caught Joanna in a tight embrace. She slowly wrapped her arms around him. Usually, she was not the hugging type, but something about his hug made her warm and gooey on the inside.

"Got to go," Ricky said. "It was nice to meet you, Joanna."

In a brief moment, he went off running. Joanna waved goodbye. She left the park with a little tickle in her stomach and a gleaming smile upon her face.

When she got to the bus stop, she searched her pockets for her pass. She checked the right; it wasn't there. She checked the left, nothing. She checked the inside of her coat. She checked everywhere. Everything was empty. No phone, no wallet.

"Ah, shit," she groaned, curling her hands into fists.

Moral of the story - beware of pickpockets; they come in all shapes and sizes.

About the Author

Michael Bril was born in Brazil to missionary parents and spent the first few years of his life living on the road. Being home schooled from an early age, he lived rather secluded up until college. Stories and novels gave him inspiration and a drive toward adventure.

The Café

Megan Duarte

"Love isn't something you find.

Love is something that finds you."

Loretta Young

The first night it happened, I didn't pay much attention. I was far too caught up in a book I was reading, and truthfully, I'm not big on socializing with strangers.

Every Tuesday night, I went to my favorite café that was down the street from my apartment, so often that it became a routine for me.

It was a quaint little café, and I enjoyed it mostly because of the privacy waiting there. No one ever bothered me, and it seemed apparent that no one there wanted to be bothered either. So to me, it was perfect.

Well, it was, until I started to get bothered.

It all happened so suddenly. I wasn't even too sure what to think of it. A plastic cup and a small piece of paper slid towards me with only a slight nod from a barista telling me it was from a young gentleman.

At first, I didn't really know what to think of it, so I ignored it by shoving the note in my bag and just enjoying the coffee.

The second time it happened, I was just as shocked, but again I ignored it and continued with my book.

The third time it happened, however, I started getting a little suspicious. Who on earth was repeatedly sending me these drinks with a note?

I scanned the café, looking for anyone who looked out of the ordinary, or even someone who just caught my eye, determined to find the sender.

The room was filled with mostly older women and men who looked deep in work and the occasional group of teenage girls giggling over something with each other. Was it possible that he had already left?

I could have very well just read the note to maybe get a clue of whom he was, but I refused to be pestered by some secret admirer or something. I simply needed to find out who he was and kindly tell him that I appreciated the gesture, but I was not interested. Simple right?

Not exactly.

As time went on, the drinks and the notes continued, week after week, and each week, I became more agitated. Wasn't the person taking a hint?

After some time, I stopped acknowledging the drinks altogether, and as soon as I would receive the drink, I would kindly push it back to the barista and ask if he could possibly reuse it instead. The notes, however, I kept, still curious as to what they entailed, but not curious enough to open and read them.

One particular night, I decided to invite my close friend to tag along with me, simply to catch up, but also as a sort of experiment. I was curious as to whether or not the sender would still send me something knowing I wasn't alone, or just stop altogether. Truthfully, I was hoping he would stop.

My friend and I conversed for a while, getting into our conversation, and of course, when the time came, a drink was slid over to me with the note following.

"Damn it." I muttered, scowling at them.

"Wait. What is this? Who is it from?"

"I wish I knew. Every Tuesday night when I'm here, this always happens. I get a drink and a note; never fails. I've tried everything to get it to stop and even tried looking for whoever is sending it, but I always come up short. I don't know what to do about it anymore."

"Have you tried asking the baristas?"

"Yes, and they're just as clueless. Or, they're helping protect whoever it is. They probably want me to find out on my own."

"Well, what do the notes say?"

"Oh, I don't know. I never read them."

"What? Why not?"

"I don't know. I kind of just don't want to feed into the madness. I feel that once I read the notes, it will get worse somehow."

"Well, it's up to you. You could either read the notes to get some closure, or you can ignore it altogether and hope it stops. Personally, I think you should just read them. For all you know, the guy could be some creep!"

"Well, that's promising." I laughed. "But, I'm still not sure. I just want to see how long he can keep this up."

"Well, since you're not budging, I'm just going to go ahead and enjoy this coffee, might as well go to some use."

I laughed.

****

For the past few weeks, my friend's advice had been running through my mind nonstop. I was currently sitting in the café with the notes spread out on the table in front of me, debating what to do. I was listing the pros and cons of opening the notes in my mind, and so far, the pros were winning.

I mean they couldn't be that bad, right?

I grabbed one from the top, turning it over in my hands, trying to find the courage to open it. I took a deep breath and finally just opened it, noticing the messy writing first. Inside was a poem, four lines with a scraggly signature at the bottom.

Honestly, I didn't know much about poetry. I've never been big on it, and I often have a hard time detecting the meaning behind them, but this one in particular stood out to me because of the clear meaning I felt was demonstrated through it.

I reread it, absorbing the words in my mind. Then, I quickly grabbed another note hoping it contained another poem. As I opened it, I grew excited to see another and before I knew it, I was scouring through the pile to read every one.

Exactly a half hour later, I had finally finished reading every note, completely absorbed by each beautifully written poem. I was so caught up in rereading them all that I nearly missed the drink and note that were slid my way, completely forgetting that I had arrived early to the café that day. I greedily grabbed the note, disregarding the drink, and opened it to my disappointment only to see a few numbers and a street name.

Why did he decide to give me an address now of all times?

I slowly gathered my things, gathering all the notes into a small pile and shoving them into the pocket of my jacket, clutching the note I just received in my hand. Luckily, I recognized the street name as being close by. Otherwise, I wouldn't have gone, fearing I would've walked into a bad neighborhood.

When I arrived, I saw that the address led me to a small bookstore on a semi-busy street and deemed it safe enough to enter. Upon entering, I felt as if I had been sent into a movie scene with how marvelous the bookstore was. There were books upon books stacked on shelves in the walls, a large waterfall-looking piece that had books in place of the water, frozen in place to create an illusion of never-ending books.

I stared in wonder of how beautiful the place was. I felt as though I could get lost in the place, surrounded by so many books. I glanced at a shelf, running my fingers along the various titles in awe of the place.

"Need any help?"

I turned around only to see a young guy around my age with messy brown hair and hazel eyes, and I almost ogled at how attractive he was.

"No I, um, was just looking around. This place is wonderful."

"Thanks, I'm glad you like it."

"What's not to like? Anyways, I actually came here to find something, well someone in particular," I said, walking towards the center of the store.

"And did you find what you were looking for?" He asked, leading me to the front desk. He stopped once behind it, leaning forward on his elbows. I glanced around the desk, seeing various notebooks and a plastic cup lying on it and immediately noticed something that caught my eye.

"I think I did."

He smiled.

About the Author

Megan Duarte is an aspiring author from Southern California who enjoys writing and crafting in her spare time. She has been writing stories ever since she was a freshman in high school and has continued ever since. Now a full-time college student, she resides in California where she hopes to one day start her own business.

Wondering

Clarissa Flowers

The first hello is like the last goodbye, for we all hope for new beginnings and fresh starts. For every start, there is an end. That makes us wonder the possibilities of happiness. Even though they are both hard to say, we still find hope within those words, no matter how much of it is uncertain.

Clarissa Flowers

Possibilities are the most likely chances, to be or not to be. For many years, Kim and Jeff have always wondered if their love was meaningful, or was it a moment in life that they should just treasure?

Jeff was a tall six foot five man that weighed 187 pounds of pure bones and hazelnut skin. He had the most contagious smile that could make birds sing and the sun shine on the most depressing day. His smile was something you anticipated but would rarely see. His eyes looked like brown glass marbles that glistened in all colors of light. With a lack of emotion or feelings, he came off as very mean and intimidating, until he met Kimmy, the weirdo, the last semester of their senior year of high school.

"Grrr, ruff, ruff, grr," Kim barked at Jeff, as if she was a big dog, while walking past him with a playful smirk waiting for a reaction. She stood five foot four with thick black wild curly hair. Her hair was so wild; it looked like she had stuck her fingers in an electrical plug. She had the complexion of a milk chocolate candy bar. Jeff could not resist; he unexpectedly barked back and smiled.

The bell had rung, so it was time to go to class from lunch. That moment became the start of something new, for the both of them; that was unexplainable. The next day at lunch, they both walked past each other with a lot to say but watched one another with a blank stare. Kim did not understand what had just happened, but she realized something had changed in her spirit.

Hours, days, and weeks went by, and they still did not speak. "Jahhhy...Michel Riches ..." the principle called out for students to come up and receive their diplomas. He finally called Kim's name. As she scanned the sea of people to look for her parents, she could only spot Jeff. As she walked down the stairs, he barked at her, and all she could do was laugh.

When it was his turn to receive his diploma, she howled. After the graduation ceremony, Kim went looking for her parents, and they were nowhere to be found. Her eyes immediately became glossy, her nose began to sting, and tears filled her eyes. As the first tear began to form, she heard a voice say, "My name is Jeff." Jeff then recited from the movie _22 Jump Street_.

Kim began to laugh, and she formally introduced herself, forgetting that her parents did not show. Even though she was laughing and joking around, Jeff knew she was sad. They exchanged numbers and said their good byes.

Every time Jeff would call, it seemed as if Kim's line was busy, or she was always gone. He began to think, *What if she does not like me, or maybe it's the wrong number.* Jeff became sad and emotional as if his world stopped. But then, his phone rang; it was Kim. It was like a weight lifted off his chest. He was ecstatic to hear her voice. They began to hang out often to the point that they both wondered if they should consider a relationship.

Things began to change suddenly... "I'm calling you to see if... you are okay ... How's everything going? I miss you ... Ummh, I know it is only been a week and a half, but yeah call me back," Jeff said to Kim's answering machine.

Kim was lost in her own little world. Her grandmother had died earlier that week, and she did not know how to handle it. Kim had never a lowed people to see her cry, and she never planned to. She always hid from the world and only cried at night, so no one would hear her. During the day, she would console her mother and take care of the house duties. Kim had forgotten about Jeff.

Then, as she was watching a T.V commercial about dogs, she then realized she had not talked to the one person who could make her smile. She called, and he answered the phone on the first ring. Kim was so excited to hear his voice that her eyes begin to tear up. But suddenly, Jeff rushed her off the phone because his mom just told him his dad had died.

****

Days, months, and seasons went by, and Kim called and texted him every moment she got. She then started to worry if he was okay. Was his family okay? How did his father die?

Kim called one afternoon, and they talked about the events in their lives, and they both decided to stay good friends. Deep down inside, Kim was upset because she did not want to be just his friend. Jeff knew she did not really want to be friends, but it was not working out, and in that moment in their lives, they were not ready to be in a relationship.

Their conversations became boring; it was as though there was nothing to talk about. At times, they would just hold the phone for hours. He would always make an effort to see her, but it came to the point they didn't talk much. The next time she saw him, he had a girlfriend. Kim was hurt. Her heart felt like glass being shattered, but she knew it was time to move on.

Three years later, Kim moved to New York. She wondered if what she and Jeff had was just puppy love or if she was just crazy. She did not understand how a person could just let go so fast. She went into a coffee shop where she had seen a little boy that made her cry because he looked like Jeff.

As she walked to the cashier, she felt a familiar presence. A man tapped her on back saying, "My name is Jeff." When she turned around, they both looked puzzled as if it were high school again. They talked for several hours in the coffee shop. Jeff talked about how his life had changed and how he was about to get married.

****

"Will you take.... to be...?" were the last words to be said by the pastor as Jeff and his future wife stood at the altar. Jeff was very emotional, as he looked Kim in the eye and said, "I do." Then, he realized the girl he really loved was just a guest. Kim and Jeff lived separate lives wondering what if they had gotten married.

About the Author

Clarissa Janay Flowers was born February 8, 1996. She believes there is beauty in tragedy. Her mind is full of imagination and endless thoughts. As a child, she always had questions about life. She would ask the most obvious questions just to see if others would answer them differently. Growing up, she lived in many different areas and has learned all people have problems, and people deal with things in their own way. She understands it is not wise to expect people to be or react like you. We are all created differently.

However, she loves people and expressing her emotions.

Crossing Each Other's Paths

Yadira Fuentes

"That their hearts might be comforted, being knit together in love, and unto all riches of the full assurance of understanding, to the acknowledgement of the mystery of God, and of the Father, and of Christ."

Colossians 2:2 (KJV)

On a gloomy stormy cloucy afternoon, Julian saw a young beautiful woman standing underneath a vivid green tree. The tree was surrounded by roses, gifts, and letters. Julian stopped and asked the young woman if she was okay. The young woman responded to him and said she was doing just fine. While she was responding, a tear dropped down past her rosy pink cheeks. Julian then asked the girl if she would like to come to his place until the storm passed by. The young woman was scared to be on the streets during the storm, so she told him she would love to go to his place.

Julian and the young woman were slowly driving to his home while listening to the radio. While they were in the car, Julian asked the young woman for her name, and she responded saying, "Faith." Julian was curious to know more about her, but he did not want to seem like he was trying to get into her business.

Next, Julian and Faith arrived to Julian's two-story brown house. They entered through a huge shimmery glass door. As they are going in, Faith saw several beautiful portraits on the walls. The portraits on the walls were of Julian and a gorgeous woman. The woman in the portraits had dark brown hair, soft tan skin, glowing brown eyes, light pink cheeks, and a big glowing smile. The portraits were everywhere Faith looked. Faith became curious about who the beautiful mysterious woman was. But, she just walked in without asking any questions.

Julian and Faith started a conversation as they were having hot chocolate with marshmallows. They were laughing and almost cried because of how hard they were laughing. Julian and Faith continued to get to know each other and were having a good time.

Then, much later came, and Julian was still curious. He wanted to know why she was standing alone underneath the vivid tree. Julian asked Faith questions. Faith just stared at him, and she started answering his questions. She said that was the location where her husband, Emmanuel had died. Emmanuel died in a car collision four years ago on a rainy stormy day. Julian was shocked and felt the pain Faith must have been feeling inside her chest. Julian apologized and tried changing the subject.

Faith was all right talking about the situation to Julian because she felt like she could open up to him. Then, she started telling him the story about how it happened. Faith had said it all started when

Emmanuel was coming from work late one night. Emmanuel was running a little late, more than usual, because it was their tenth year anniversary; he had stopped at the florist to buy Faith's favorite flowers and chocolates. Much later came and Faith had started to get worried.

The next thing she knew, there was a knock at the front door. She went to see who it was, and there was a police officer asking her if she was Faith. Her heart dropped, and she started to feel a hurting pain in her chest. The police officer told her that her husband was dead. He had died in a car collision. The collision was by the vivid green tree where she was standing earlier that afternoon when Julian had seen her. Julian then started to shed tears.

Next, Faith asked Julian why he was crying. Julian started to tell his story. Julian said three years ago his wife Yadira had died also in a car collision. Faith felt horrible; she felt the very same pain Julian must have been feeling. They both lost a loved one and would never see them again. Julian told Faith all the portraits on the walls were of his wife. He said when he looks at these portraits it makes him feel like Yadira was still here with him.

Julian started to tell Faith about the night his wife died. His wife was coming home to tell Julian about the great news she had. Julian had prepared dinner because she said it was going to be a special night for both of them. Julian sat and waited for Yadira to hear the great news she had for them. Julian waited and waited until he fell asleep; he woke up and became worried that his wife had never arrived.

The next thing he knew, Julian received a call on the house phone. Julian answered, and it was a doctor from the emergency room. The doctor told him that his wife was in a serious car accident, and she was rushed here in an ambulance, but when they got there his wife's heart had stop beating. The doctor also said Yadira lost the baby. Julian was devastated. The great news Yadira had for them was her pregnancy. Faith felt heartbroken to hear Julian's story. Faith was surprised how two strangers had so much in common and had experienced almost the exact same tragedy.

Finally, Julian and Faith were glad they crossed each other's paths. They continued to keep talking that night. Julian turned on the television to hear about the storm. The news weather reporter said the storm was all cleared up and it should be bright and sunny the next morning. Faith was glad the storm had passed and asked Julian if he could get her home. Julian then took her home and told her that he was glad he had met her. Faith smiled; she was glad Julian had invited her over.

Days passed, and Julian and Faith could not stop thinking about each other. Julian wanted to see Faith again. He looked up her phone number in the yellow pages. It took him a while to find her, but he did. Julian dialed Faith, and her soft sweet voice answered saying, "Hello?" Julian and Faith agreed to meet up and talk, so they did.

They met, and they both let out their emotions. They agreed they could not live without each other. Faith and Julian started dating. Julian's and Faith's relationship was going great and was getting stronger every day. No one could break the special bond they had. Julian then proposed three years later. Faith was so deep in love. She said, "Yes!" Julian and Faith got married on the date they had crossed each other's paths.

****

Years and years have passed now, and Julian and Faith have two kids. Julian and Faith are renewing their wedding vows. Most importantly, Julian and Faith are happy God brought them together.

About the Author

Yadira Fuentes is nineteen years old and was born on February 11, 1996, in San Bernardino, CA. She is a student attending Crafton Hills College She is the first in her family to attend college. Yadira enjoys watching romantic love movies, and she had never thought of writing her own love story until now.

Yadira is a passionate loving person and will go to the extreme for the people she loves. In Yadira's free time, she enjoys watching her boyfriend Julian

Sinegal play basketball, loves watching *The Walking Dead*, and loves worshiping Jesus Christ, her savior.

A Football Life

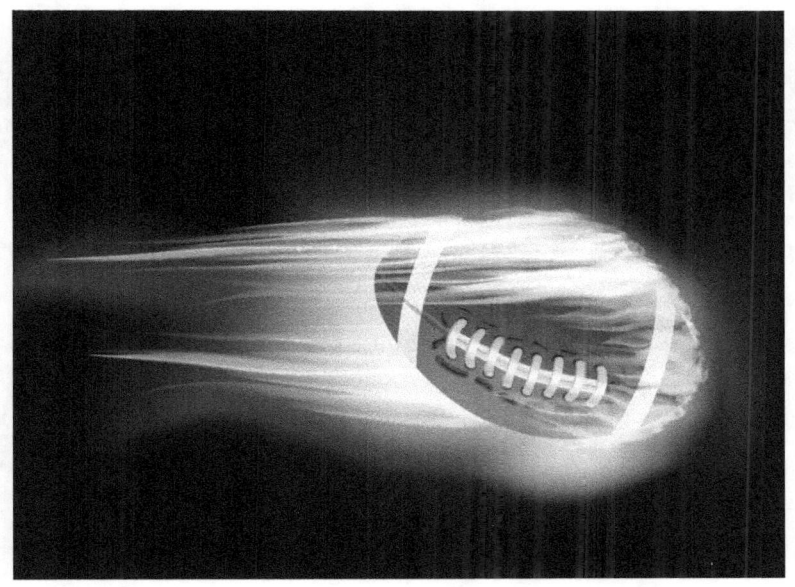

Gavin Keays

"You do have your moments. Not many, but you have them."

Star Wars

As a baby boy, Gavin was born into a baseball life. Gavin's family supported him with anything he did, even when he started playing baseball. He would play this sport until he was twelve years old. He did play one year of football when he was ten years old where he made an All American All-Star team. But, he thought he should stay with his roots, which was baseball. Then the idea of football came back up when his eighth grade year was coming to a close. His mom convinced him to try football one more time to see if he would like it. Gavin questioned the idea, but he realized his mom had made good decisions for him in the past. This started his career of football at Redlands East Valley High School. Freshmen year was the start of his life with the sport he realized he was meant to play for the rest of his high school experience.

Freshmen year consisted of more learning experiences than anything else in that school year for Gavin. He started it off with summer workouts for football that brought him to know that football was the sport for him. He actually did not start his first week of football because he was on vacation the week prior in Mexico. Gavin was actually pretty good at the sport;

he would start on the offensive line as the center and was one of the biggest players on the team. He captained for some of the games because of how he performed at practice that week, because it was a tradition to do so.

Coaches noticed his size and strength. One day, the varsity football coach asked if his father was taller, but the coach was disappointed to hear that Gavin was indeed taller than his father. The season ended with an overall record of 5-5, with the team winning half the games and losing the rivalry game, which was heartbreaking.

After the freshmen season was over, Gavin started the offseason training for the varsity season. He went through a lot of intense training from the start of February to the first day of spring ball. During all of these offseason workouts, the varsity coach would get frustrated with his class and said they were the weakest freshmen class in the years of his experience. This would make the freshmen think they needed to try harder to prove themselves to the varsity coach.

After the two weeks of spring ball, Gavin was the second string center to the senior that started his junior year. Then the extensive wait for summer training to start had begun. The young man then had to wait for July to come and to start the amazing experience of his football career.

Sophomore year started off with the extremely hard task to get through the summer workout. Players would say that week was Hell month, instead of Hell week. That month, Gavin went through so much pain and mental breakdown, which would help him grow stronger after it is all done. He got through the many workouts and still kept his spot of second string on the offensive line.

Once the season came around, he had many opportunities to play and get varsity play first hand. He would play in four games and get the coaches to see him in action. His team would beat a nationally ranked team that was third in the state and ranked tenth in the nation; this team was Mission Viejo High School that had alumni like Mark Sanchez. The team would also win the Citrus Belt League Title for the third year in a row.

They did play a championship game for the league title, which was a total massacre with the final score of 49-0 against Yucaipa High School. The season was over after his team lost in the second round of playoffs to Rancho Cucamonga, after going 11-1 and going undefeated in the regular season. This gave Gavin a light that he wanted to catch to start his junior year. He would have to catch it during spring ball to start on the offensive line. The coaches thought he was not ready to play, so they brought in a defensive lineman to start over him. Gavin would then strive to get better and show his coaches that he could play, but he would have to wait for summer workout to start again.

Junior year did not start off like sophomore year at all. The team was not as good as his sophomore year, so that meant very little playing time. Gavin only would play in three games, which only one of them he was part of two plays because of him being a long snapper for PAT's. The team finished 6-4, losing to some of the best teams of the state. They would win the Citrus Belt League Title again for a fourth year in a row, which had never happened before in the league's history. His team would lose to Norco in the first round of the playoffs.

That was an embarrassing loss with a final score of 59-24. It was an experience that brought him to realize that you cannot win every game and cannot play in every one of them either. That did not ruin his spirt to play; he kept on working to get better every day. His spirit had more confidence from a really good and inspiring coach who was the offensive coordinator for the next season. He coached at Los Osos High before coming to REV, so he had experience behind him. After junior year season was over, it was time to start the process all over again to see what he could do to play and to see if he had the chance to bring something to his team.

Beginning of senior started off at spring ball, which Gavin thought he did really well at by showing the coaches what he could do. When summer workouts started, he had a lot of confidence and the mentality to do better. He was put on second string again, which was very discouraging to him as a senior and to be a backup to a junior as a left guard. He would get through summer and begin the season as a backup, but the first game changed his mindset. The starting center got hurt on one of the plays, which would keep him off the field for three weeks. He would practice behind the starting center to get reps just in case of that problem.

That gave Gavin an opportunity to show the coaches. He played for the second half, and he thought he did pretty good to not be ready to play that game. The next week for some reason, the coaches thought differently. They thought he was still not ready for varsity ball and put another senior in front of him to start the next game. They would lose that game to St. Bonaventure 35-14 due to not having an offense from bad snaps by the center. Gavin was furious about the issue. He put all the time and effort to be ready to play and actually start. That caused more frustration within Gavin. Even after that horrible lost to a team that they could have beaten, there were more loses to Mission Viejo, Vista Murrieta, and Orange Lutheran, which were games where his team had total control but lost it due to the starting quarterback getting injured. Nothing would happen until rival week, which they incorporated a heavy set of linemen for a formation.

He was one of the three linemen for that for-mation. That formation would be used many times in the rival game against Redlands High School. That brought little happiness to Gavin, but the damage had already been done to his self-esteem. He would play in the last two games, but they were both losses to Eisenhower and Rancho Cucamonga in the first round of the CIF playoff. Those would be his last games ever to play for his school's football program. His team would win another Citrus Belt title for a fifth year in a row. He put all that time to just be treated like he was nothing.

To this very day, he is still not happy for what his coaches did not see in him and what they did not understand about what they did to him mentally.

Gavin would get over his anger that year, but that frustration with his coaches will forever be with him. That was just him trying to show he is worth something to the program and to be a proud alumnus for his school. In all of his anger and frustration, Gavin still had an amazing time with his team and coaches. He never thought about passing all of those memories up for anything.

****

He is a proud alumnus for his high school for winning CIF from a lower division and also winning the Division II State Championship. He knew everybody in that class and on that team, which brought him happiness for his fellow teammates.

Deep down, he was happy and would never change his experience from his four years on that team of brothers. The love of the sport gave him all the strength he needed to be successful and to have the best experience of his life.

About the Author

Gavin Keays was born at Loma Linda hospital and was raised in Highland, California during his youth. He then moved to Redlands, California for high school, where he attended Redlands East Valley High School. He graduated with the class of 2014 and now attends Crafton Hills College.

A Day to Remember

Karen Lopez

"A mother's love is forever; time, distance, hardship... all fall before the strength of her love."
Unknown

It was 6:00 am, and Sandra could hear the wind blowing outside of her mobile home. She quickly turned the television on and heard the news reporter say Hurricane Rita was fast approaching Houston, TX, and everyone needed to quickly evacuate to the nearest city. She knew staying there was not safe for her and her kids, so she decided to pack her most important belongings and drive to the nearest city.

As Sandra drove away from her home, she could see the trees move from side to side. She knew right away Hurricane Rita was coming fast and strong. The thought of possibly losing her home because of the hurricane ran across Sandra's mind. She knew if that happened, she would have to start all over again. In the end, nothing was more important to her than the safety of her kids.

When Sandra got on the freeway, she came across horrible traffic. It seemed that everyone like her had decided to evacuate and leave their homes behind. The cars seemed to not be moving at all, and everyone was just stuck on the freeway.

Even though the wind was blowing fast and strong, the temperature outside was sticky and very hot. Sandra could feel the sweat dripping down her neck, so she decided to roll down all the windows of her car. At first, she wanted to put the A/C on, but she heard on the radio that none of the gas stations nearby had any petroleum, so she knew she had to save as much gas as she could. After being on the freeway for nearly twelve hours, Sandra barely made it to a city named Katy. She wished she could just stay there, but it was said that every shelter and hotel was completely full. Her plan was to eventually arrive in San Antonio.

As she was driving, she turned around to see how her kids were doing, and she noticed her youngest son Danny wasn't really breathing, and his arms were covered in hives. Sandra immediately pulled over and opened the door where Danny was. She took him out of the car and asked him what was wrong. Danny didn't respond because the lack of breathing wouldn't let him talk.

She asked Danny to open his mouth, and she noticed most of his tongue was swollen. When Sandra saw that, she knew she had to act fast and call an ambulance because her son could completely stop breathing at any moment. She called the ambulance and explained to them what was going on. They said they would try their best and get there as fast as they could, but because of how packed the freeway was, it was not going to be easy.

Sandra waited for the ambulance, but they seemed to be taking forever to get to her location. The entire time Sandra waited, she noticed her son being able to breathe less and less. The thought of her son dying made her extremely sad, and it also made her start panicking. She knew she had to control herself because her other son was also there, and she did not want to worry him more than he already was.

Finally after twenty minutes of waiting, the ambulance arrived. They immediately put an oxygen mask on Danny and loaded him into the back of the ambulance. Sandra and her other son also got in the back of the ambulance and were told they were going to take Danny to the children's hospital in San Antonio, TX. On the way to the children's hospital, Sandra could see that Danny was finally able to start breathing a little bit more. When she saw that, she felt like a weight was lifted off her.

When they finally arrived to the children's hospital in San Antonio, they immediately took Danny out of the ambulance and rushed him inside. The doctors took a close look at Danny and examined him. After hours of doing tests and blood work, they explained to Sandra that Danny had had a very bad allergic reaction to something. They weren't a hundred percent sure what had caused it, but Danny was lucky to be alive. At that moment, Sandra realized how lucky she was to still have her son alive. The doctor suggested for Danny to stay at the hospital for the rest of the night, so they could make sure he was fully recovered. Sandra went to the waiting room with her other son and saw that the news was on. She turned up the volume on the television and heard the news reporter say Hurricane Rita had finally arrived to Houston, TX.

A week went by and Sandra had finally decided to return home. She drove to Houston not knowing what she was going to find when she got home. Many thoughts ran through her head. Had she lost her home? Was she going to have to start all over again? She didn't know what to expect, but she knew she had to mentally prepare herself for the worst.

When she turned onto her street, she saw that her mobile home was completely destroyed. All of her belongings were wet and scattered all over the street. She turned around and saw tears inside of her kids' eyes. She immediately hugged them and told them everything was going to be alright, that the important thing was that they were all together and safe.

About the Author

Karen Lopez was born in Montclair, California, on January 7, 1993. She is the eldest of three children and is of Mexican descent. By the age of two, her family decided to move to Houston, Texas. She was raised there until the age of twelve, and then she and her family relocated to California. She currently resides in Redlands, CA and is a full-time student at Crafton Hills College. Her major is yet to be determined. In her spare time, she enjoys reading, writing and educating herself about cosmetology.

The Dreams of Two Lovers

Stacey Ogden

As daylight crept through the blinds, it caused the girl to awaken from her slumber. She lingered there awake while she replayed the dream she had over and over again in her head. The dream was of a young man. She had just seen him for the first time. In her dream, she felt such closeness to this young man, a man she had never met. She felt separated from him when she awoke.

She was only fifteen years old, but in the dream, she was a woman. The man was very close to her age. In her dream, the two of them were in tune with one another. They were in an open field rolling around in tall blades of grass on a warm summer day. They stopped their playfulness for a moment and just gazed into each other's eyes. There was a feeling of calm in their world and peace in the depths of their souls. It was a sweet dream.

For the girl, that place of peace and lovingness was only a dream at that point in her life. It was a sweet but distant dream. She tried and tried to make herself fall back into the tranquil dream, wishing to once again meet up with the man. She felt like she knew him so well. As she lay in bed, she thought to herself, *Who is this man?* She couldn't quite remember what the man looked like, except those piercing green eyes, eyes she could gaze into for an eternity.

Her mind wondered. She pondered the thought of someone having similar dreams of her. She wondered if the man were real. Little did she know that the man in her dream was having the same vivid dreams of her. He was only fifteen years old when the dreams started for him too. He felt the same closeness, comfort, and joy as the girl did. He would sit and wonder about the woman daily, what she may be doing, what she may be like, and if she knew he was thinking about her.

As time went on, they both grew older. They lived thousands of miles away from each other. Even with city's separating them, they were drawn to each other. Day by day, inch by inch, the world would work in their favor bringing them closer and closer together. Their magnetic bond could not be broken. In fact, it only grew stronger with time.

Twelve years later, the magnetic pull brought them together. At that time, they were not just together in their dreams. They were brought together in the flesh.

Between the years from their childhood until then, they had never stopped thinking about one another. Somehow, they both knew they would end up with one another. The only questions were when and where they would meet. That was never certain.

The girl moved from city to city. She could never stay put in one town. She was on a journey. She didn't understand why. She just went where her heart told her to go. It was as though she was just passing through towns and cities. As she grew older, her time spent in each town became shorter and shorter. It was as if she realized he was not there. And so, she moved on to the next city. Each move gradually brought her a little closer to him. Then finally, the world made it clear to her she must stay. By that time, she was so used to moving, it was hard for her to adjust to staying in one place.

She felt a connection to that place. She wasn't certain what it was. She had been there before, but that time it was different. They both knew they were close to one another, but they had no real idea what the other looked like, other than their eyes.

They eventually found each other. They met in passing, through colleagues. Neither of them realized that the other was the person they had been dreaming of and searching for all of those years. They would talk, but not much more than a kind hello.

Until one day she announced she was leaving again. She was planning a journey to the other side of the world. She was planning on coming back, but she planned to travel abroad for as long as she could. Then it hit him... That may be the girl I have been waiting and longing for all these years. He thought it was time. He began to seek her out. They spoke briefly before she left. He wanted to make it known that he would be waiting for her to return. And he did wait patiently for her. He waited for her to call or write, but she never did. He was afraid she would never come back. He didn't know if he would ever hear from her again.

Finally, after her travels, she made it back home. He had been in her thoughts more and more. She contacted him to let him know that she was back safely, and that it would be nice to see him. He was relieved. They decided to have dinner.

When he picked her up, they were both nervous. Their hearts was racing, and their knees were trembling. Then, their eyes met. For the first time, each of them knew they were looking into the eyes they had dreamed of. They started talking, and everything seemed to fall into place. They were so natural together. The attraction was genuine and mutual. Gradually, they fell into a deep love. The love they felt grew as they spent more and more time together.

Jealous outsiders felt they needed to challenge their love. The outsiders did not understand what had driven them together. They did not understand the closeness the lovers shared. They started feeding the young woman doubt and words of anger towards the young man. They wanted nothing less than the man out of her life. They had their reasons, some selfish, some not. The young woman heard their words and challenged the man.

He was a man of honor. In time, the woman realized that. That was when the women realized that he was truly the man she had been dreaming about. Their foundation was formed in the chaos. The challenges of their world helped them to grow stronger as individuals and as lovers. Her love for him deepened.

When the dust settled and the onlookers were silenced, the lovers looked deep into each other's hearts. What they found was perfect compatibility. She knew that he was the exact person she had been searching for. She knew he would be the perfect partner. He felt the same about her. Their lives were meant to be spent with each other.

As time went on, they grew old together. The man grew old, and so did the woman. Their love was eternal. They knew their souls would be connected forever. Their bodies would eventually die, but they didn't have any need for their bodies. They were able to let go knowing that. They trusted the same energy that brought them together in their youth would hold them together eternally.

The man was the first to leave this world. As he passed away, he stared into the woman's eyes deeply. Those eyes were a piercing deep blue, and she stared back lovingly into his, thinking back to all the memories they shared in their lifetime. She knew that she did not want to live in a world without his love and shortly passed away to join him.

About the Author

Stacey Ogden is currently a freshman at College of the Desert. This is her second published writing, and she is proud to share them with you. She is planning a lifetime of learning.

THE MAN
AND
THE QUEEN

Zak O'Mara

"In three words, I can sum up everything I've learned about life: It goes on."

Robert Frost

A man found himself seated alone at a park; the day was overcast, a reflection of his mood, setting the scene as bleak and miserable as only a heart-shattering day could be. His mind was filled by contemplation as to where he went wrong. He let the flowers he brought fall to the ground... she hadn't wanted them anyway. What did the flowers matter now? -- They didn't.

Holding his head in his hands, he played through past conversations and events over and over again trying to find the exact moment when he made the defining mistake in his relationship, every small misstep slowly growing into regret. Upon further introspection, he began to hate himself for each character flaw he could find, and even his most admirable features soon became worthy of scorn.

"Hey! You!" a shrill, high-pitched voice shouted.

The man looked up and around. The imminent rain rendered the park deserted, and there was no person to be seen.

"You, weepy man! I'm over here!"

The man looked in the direction of the voice. He saw a chessboard; it was on a picnic table a few yards away. He stood and cautiously walked to the table. Once in front of it, the voice sounded again.

"There you go; now look down."

The man looked downwards as instructed and saw that the black queen had fallen off the chessboard, off of the table, and onto the ground and now lay just before his feet.

"Did you just speak to me?" said the man, picking up the piece. It was ornate, a figure of a beautiful queen seated upon a throne.

"Yes, you fool," said the queen. "Now if you would be so kind as to return me to H6, that was my last position before I was knocked off the board." Seeing his hesitation, she explained.

"Place me on the chessboard on the black space to the immediate left of the white knight... now!" The man hastily placed the queen where she had commanded.

"Thank you," she said.

"No problem," he said, slightly confused about what had just happened. "I've never met a talking chess piece before."

"Well, now you have. Good day." Thusly being dismissed, the man turned to leave. Shaking off the absurdity of what just happened, his mind returned to thoughts about his ill-fated relationship.

Seeing the piteous state of the man, the black queen said, "You're being foolish you know."

"Pardon me?" said the man, turning back to look at the chessboard. The queen turned her head towards him.

"There's a certain point where one must ask oneself, 'What is the next move in the game?'"

"What are you talking about?"

"Don't interrupt," she demanded. The man pursed his lips, suppressing his curiosity.

"You must simply *stop dwelling on the piece taken* and the strategies that will no longer work, and think of the next possible move you can make. Remember your failure, and in the future, do not put your pieces at risk. Look at every angle. Don't think of it emotionally, and contemplate every possible outcome before proceeding. Don't get hasty and do something stupid. The game doesn't stop for you just because you're feeling mopey; the game must go on to its conclusion!" She ended with a crescendo, and she and the man stared at one other for a moment.

"You may speak now," she said.

"Thank you," said the man. "I'll try to remember all of that."

"It's my move," she said and then returned to looking straight ahead, and she became once again an inanimate object. The man examined the board once more; it had been abandoned mid game. He could see the next obvious move for the queen to make. He paused to consider possible repercussions, and finding there weren't any, he moved the black queen forward, and by moving forward, he won the game.

It was checkmate, and time to start a new game.

About the Author

Zak O'Mara is a novelist, screenwriter, and playwright. His genres of writing include fantasy, fairytales, sci-fi, and horror. He began writing when he was nine years old and "hasn't skipped a day."

He currently lives in California and works as a writer and creative consultant. He also is the organizer of the Orange County Coffee House Writers Group.

Disneyland

Danyelle Pappas

6 Don't worry about anything; instead,

pray about everything.

Tell God what you need,

and thank him for all he has done.

7 Then you will experience God's peace,

which exceeds anything we can understand.

His peace will guard your hearts and minds

as you live in Christ Jesus.

Philippians 4:6-7 (NLT)

Sarah's mother lightly rubbed her head and said softly, "Sarah, it is time to wake up. We have a long day ahead of us." Sarah stretched her ten-year-old arms and legs. She jumped out of bed in excitement. She quickly started rustling through her drawers and picked the first outfit she could find. She brushed her teeth and slipped her shoes on. Her mother made her favorite meal: a peanut butter and jelly sandwich with a glass of milk. They had their bags packed, and the car was ready to go.

As always, Sarah started scanning radio stations, so eager to find a song she liked. They drove to Sarah's friend Rebecca's house two blocks over. As they pulled in front of Rebecca's house, Sarah honked the horn twice, rolled down the window, and shouted, "Rebecca, c'mon!" Sarah's mother laughed at how excited Sarah was. Rebecca came running out with her bags and gave her mother a kiss goodbye. She jumped in the backseat, slammed the door, buckled her seatbelt and shouted, "Let's get this show on the road!"

Off they went driving down the highway awaiting their destination. The girls blasted the radio and sang their favorite songs as loud as they could, while putting their heads out the windows like excited dogs. After trying to sit still for the car ride for two hours, the girls finally saw a big sign off the freeway that said "Disneyland." The girls screamed in excitement as they anxiously drove through the busy parking lot searching for a parking space.

When they finally parked, both girls hopped out of the vehicle and put their backpacks on. The suspense of waiting in line was killing the girls. Sarah's mother gave the worker their tickets, and they were finally in! The day Sarah had been waiting for was finally there! She was at the happiest place on earth! Her mother told the girls using the bathroom would be the smartest thing to do first. So, they did so.

When they came out of the bathroom, they spotted Minnie Mouse walking in and waving at people. Sarah said, "Please, Mom, can we go say hi to Minnie?" Her mother replied, "Of course, but do not run." The two girls power walked to their idol of all time. They both hugged Minnie, and Sarah's mom took a picture of the two best friends sharing their special moment. Minnie waved goodbye and walked off into the park.

Sarah was in amazement by all the Christmas decorations that were everywhere. There were big red bows on the light poles, greenery stretching from one pole to the next covered in Christmas lights. The little shops were outlined with Christmas lights and fake snow fell from above. The girls were in heaven. Sarah's mother grabbed a map, and they decided to start their adventure. First, they went through all the Disney character's houses: Goofy's, Mickey's, and Minnie's. Their houses looked like they came right out of the TV show.

They then decided to go to the next nearest thing on the map, which was the "Winnie the Pooh" ride. The theme of the ride was Winnie the Pooh's dream, so it was dark inside, and the characters and figures had a bright glow to them. After that, they decided to go on a new ride called "A Nightmare before Christmas." That line was longer than others, so the girls were not thrilled. Sarah's mother tried to keep them occupied by playing a game of "I Spy." The girls enjoyed looking for a man with a beard, a baby crying, and a woman with colored hair. The challenge made time go by fast for the girls, and before they knew it, they were at the front of the line!

The ride was very dark inside and spooky music was playing to add effect to the theme of the ride. When they finally got off the ride, they rushed out of the gates looking for what they were going to do next.

The cool breeze brought a pleasant smell to the ladies' noses. Sarah looked at her mother and said, "Please, Mom, please! The smell of that funnel cake is calling my name!" Sarah's mother gave her a look and said, "Okay girls, but you have to split one."

The girls anxiously ran to the stand and got in line. When it was finally their turn to order, the funnel cake was made within minutes. They sat down and embezzled the sweet treat. The next ride Maggie spotted was "The Little Mermaid." The seats only had two seats, so Sarah's mother said she'd wait outside for them. The seats they sat in during the ride were in the shape of seashells. The ride led them through all of the famous scenes from the movie. The girl's sang along to the song "Under the Sea" playing throughout the ride duration.

After the ride, Sarah's mom noticed on the map that the parade was going to start soon. The three of them walked to where the parade was and tried to get as close as possible. In the parade, the first thing they saw were people dressed as nutcrackers playing musical instruments. The first float was covered in fake snow and had a gigantic Christmas tree. Donald Duck and Daisy were dancing on the float and waving to everyone.

The next part Maggie loved; Winnie the Pooh was on a rocking chair, and Tigger was riding a sled. Each character had fake snow under them and their individual seat had wheels, so they were moving from left to right. Women dressed in white with big sparkly snowflakes on their backs were skating all around. The characters everyone had been waiting for finally surprised the crowd. Mickey and Minnie came walking out waving at everyone. Minnie had a red and white Christmas dress on, while Mickey had a suit and tie. Sarah's mom was ecstatic to see her all-time favorite Disney characters.

Then last but not least, Santa Claus rode in a big glamorous sleigh. Once the parade was wrapped up, the girls were exhausted from the long adventure they had. Walking to the car was not fun with the big crowds of people. Sarah's mom made the two girls hold hands, so they would not get lost. Once they finally made it to the car, everyone buckled up and got cozy.

Sarah's mom asked her, "Was Disneyland what you hoped it to be?"

Sarah replied," It was beyond what I expected! Definitely the happiest place on earth!"

Sarah's mother smiled in satisfaction; she was happy to make Sarah's dream come true.

About the Author

Danyelle is currently a Youth Development Professional at Boys and Girls Club. She lives in Banning, California. She attends Crafton Hills College in hopes of becoming an elementary school teacher one day. Children are the light of her life. She enjoys writing fictional stories that are humorous and adventurous. Danyelle believes smiling is the key to happiness.

Color Theory

Kayghee Reynolds

God. Her smile

Lit up my world

It was the star

That I based

My entire life's route

I would do or

Even give anything

To keep that smile

Living on that face

Kayghee Reynolds

Sam had learned to live with her dead-end job and mediocre sex life, but she seemed to struggle with the concept that her upstairs neighbor wasn't in fact a tap dancer. I mean... Come on! The noise that came from above was awful. Every day and every night the clicking of irregular beats went on. She turned over onto her back and glared at the ceiling then at her clock. It read, in startlingly bright red: five am. There was less than an hour 'til she was supposed to get up for her day, so there was no point in struggling with sleep.

Sam's feet dangled just above the floor, as she sat on the edge of the bed. Most people would be able to reach the floor with no problem, but when you barely make it to five feet on a good day, that wasn't gonna happen. She attempted to find the hair tie in her hair buy gave up and walked to the bathroom. The light and the sight of her bird's nest hair burned her eyes..

"Mirror mirror on the wall.... Who's the sleepiest one of all?" She managed to mumble that out during a yawn and stretch. "Why am I not shocked that it's still my face in the mirror?"

With water on, clothes off and hair tie removed, she entered the shower. From there on, her morning routine stayed pretty much the same. She grabbed her tea and a stale bagel off the counter before she left out the door for work.

Her job was as a filing clerk at a small law office on the edge of town. The old man who owned the business was nice enough to tolerate but really was just a pain in the ass. Jake and Sally were two of the other office staff that weren't lawyers themselves. Sally was the go-fer (go-fer this... go-fer that...) while Jake answered all the calls and kept the calendars up to date.

"Whatcha doing?" Sally cooed as she hopped onto the shorter filing cabinet. Sam simply shook the papers at her and smiled.

"No! I mean tonight! Like, are you gonna come with Jake and me to get a few drinks?"

"Uh, sure. Where at?" Her voice always seemed to go up an octave when talking to Sally. Her violently bright eyes were very distracting.

"The pub down by Main! Oh man, this is gonna be great!" Her hair seemed to explode when she dropped back down to the ground.

142

The shift seemed to fly by, and soon they arrived for drinks. The outside had a brick facade with wooden accents, and it even came with the cliché drunk guy pissing on the wall outside. They got out of the car and walked towards the crusty-looking bar. Sally always bounced when she walked, while Jake was a floater. Two very different personality types and yet they were madly in love. She could go on for hours about the moment they met, how "green" his shirt was, or how "purple" his hair looked. Her world switched instantly from black and white to full Technicolor just like everyone else... except for Sam. She always hoped that one day when she turned the corner, she would see the full spectrum of colors. So, when she opened the door she held her breath for one second.

Nothing. Still same black carpet with middle grey bar and light grey barstools. They all pulled one out and sat down.

"What can I get for you all?" The bartender's name was Florence. He had a pretty sick beard and tattoos you would not believe.

"I'll have an Adios, Jake wants your tallest Budweiser and..." Sally turned to Sam with a stupid grin on her face that she gets when she thinks she's meeting someone new. Little did she know that they had met in high school.

"I'll have the light grey martini." Sally's eyes left hers with a disappointed glint in them.

"Nutin still huh?" Jake had a pity-for-you smile on. He felt bad because he was dating Sam when Sally showed up. Sam was hurt, sure, but she knew you couldn't help something like that. They both knew it would happen some day with someone else.

"Nope, but really it's okay. Please, let's just have a good time."

They finished round one, which was also the end for Jake who was designated driver. Sam and Sally, however, got so plastered they eventually made their way to the floor. Jake walked both giggling blobs to the car, dropped off Sam safely at home; then, took off homeward bound with Sally to sleep.

Sam immediately crawled into bed and knocked out, but around 7am she woke up to someone attempting to drill into her brain. That or a gnarly hangover plus the tapping from upstairs; she really couldn't tell at that point. Sam's eye twitched from the frustration, and she rolled out of bed. That time was the final straw; that time she was going to go up and say something! So, she threw on some shades, pulled her hair up and zombie marched upstairs. She knocked loudly on the door and waited for the dweller. Lightly padded footsteps raced towards the door, the door lock clicked, and it swung open.

Framed within the yellow doorway was a tall, slender woman with pale pink lips, flaming red locks, the deepest brown eyes and the greenest dress Sam had ever seen. Ever.

About the Author

Kayghee Reynolds is currently a student at Fullerton College and is studying psychology. She loves the outdoors and painting in her free time. Her hope is to help other people believe in themselves and see their full potential.

Her Niece

Meagen Sais

"So keep your head high. Keep your chin up and most importantly keep smiling because life's a beautiful thing and there's so much to smile about."

Marilyn Monroe

"Love at first sight" was something that she was very skeptical about. Helen felt that way because it was something that had not happened to her before. She went looking for love but always came to a dead end. Then one day, she found love but not the kind you find romantically. The first day she laid eyes on her, she then realized that love comes in many different ways. She had fallen in love from the day she was born, the day she turned a year. the day she turned two and the day she turned three. Helen loved her niece so much; there were not enough words to explain it.

Her mother Gloria, her brother-in-law Bryan, and her nine-month pregnant sister Nickole walked into the hospital hoping it was not another false alarm. They knew it was not a false alarm when they had admitted Nickole and put her in a hospital gown. It was late at night, and Helen and her mother Gloria sat patiently and anxiously waiting for some kind of news. They sat for hours until finally Bryan rushed in and stated that baby Nedia was on her way out. As they walked into the room, her sister Nickole had to only push twice and finally Nedia was born.

At that moment, Helen fell so in love with her niece. Nedia had a head full of hair and the cutest little smile ever. Helen had never seen anything more precious. The following day came, and Nickole and Nedia received visitors; one of them was Nedia's big brother Ezekiel. For the first time, Ezekiel held his baby sister, and it was definitely a precious moment. The way he looked at her was just beautiful. They all knew he was proud to be her big brother and knew he would do everything in his power to protect her.

****

About a year old, Nedia was just walking all over the place. Helen could not believe how fast she had grown. It seemed like not long ago, they were at the hospital. Nedia was then climbing down off the couches and climbing out of her pack and play.

One day, Helen was watching her, and it was about noon time, Nedia's nap time. She was fighting her sleep, so Helen decided to do what she had done when Nedia was a newborn: sing her to sleep; Nedia fell asleep within the next fifteen minutes. Watching her sleep, Helen cannot help but shed a tear of happiness thinking about how crazy it was going to be watching her grow up, with all the mistakes and heartbreaks she would go through and all the happy times and life lessons that would be coming her way.

She will be fine because Aunty Helen will be there to help out with all the advice and life experiences that Mommy just could not do, Helen thought. As she slept, she had a smile on her face, and Helen cannot help but wonder what she was dreaming about but she knew that she was happy. That was one thing that mattered most, knowing and seeing her little niece happy.

Another year passed, and Nedia was two years old. It still felt like just yesterday when she had been born. Watching her grow was such a blessing. Her mommy liked to do nails and make up, so growing up, she had been around that and that was all she ever wanted to do. If you gave her nail polish and asked her to paint your nails, she would hold your hand and paint your nails. If the paint were to get on your skin, she knew exactly how to wipe it off.

Not only did she like to do those things, she loved to go swimming. Helen called her a little fish because she could be in the pool literally all day. She loved to swim by herself. For a two year old, she was a fast learner, well sort of. She knew how to swim but not without her floaters. With them on, she could jump from the deep end and swim all the way to the three feet all by herself. So many things at the age of two Nedia's family were so proud about.

At the age of three, Nedia had learned so much. Helen was definitely one proud aunt. Nedia was determined to go to school. She noticed that her big brother Ezekiel, who by that time was in first grade, was going to school by taking the school bus. Nedia was just so fascinated by it all. One day, Ezekiel had an awards assembly and when they called his name, Nedia ran up there to him and gave him a big hug. When the new school year started and all the other kids got new backpacks, she asked where hers was.

As each year passed, it was something new, and it just amazed Helen how much Nedia grew every year. She loved her niece so much that she would do just about anything for her. Helen had not felt love in so long and for her to know how much Nedia loved her was just enough to get her by during the day.

Some people look for love because they feel lonely, but little do they know they can find love in many different ways. Helen found love by watching her niece grow up. Once she had realized that she had been loved, she never felt alone again because she knew that from miles away Nedia loved her just as much as she loved Nedia.

Whenever Helen felt sad and alone, she would just pick up the phone and call her niece, and with just that one phone call, everything ended up being perfectly fine in Helen's life. To see her smile and to hear her laugh was something Helen looked forward to every single day from the day Nedia was born.

From then, it is all Helen ever waits for. She waits for the days to pass of her learning from her mistakes to waiting for the days to come so she can help guide her in the right directions in her life. The directions that Mommy cannot direct but only an aunty can.

About the Author

Meagen is twenty-one years old and was born on October 1, 1993 in Fontana, California. She is a full-time student at Crafton Hills College. She is the first girl in her family to attend college.

Meagen loves to spend time with her family and go on spontaneous adventures. She loves to help others. She also enjoys listening to music. She does not have a specific genre; she likes to listen to everything.

THE OCEAN'S SALT WATER

Daisy Sekly

"The will of God will not take us where the grace of God cannot sustain us."

Billy Graham

There once was a small island, east of the Mediterranean Sea. It was very isolated, and the people who lived there were all very poor. The people lacked food, shelter, and resources for medication. The only thing they had a wide variety of was salt.

A fourteen-year-old girl named Alex lived on this remote island with her two younger brothers and sick mother. The mother was suffering from a severe case of pneumonia, and no one on the island knew how to help cure it. There came a day where Alex's mother grew more ill, and she was becoming weaker as the days passed by. Alex knew she had to step out of her comfort zone and do something to try to help her mother. She thought to herself, *What might there be across the sea?* No one ever sailed farther than ten feet from the island in fear of getting lost in the ocean or caught by a huge wave.

After taking matters into consideration, Alex decided it was time someone went out looking for a better opportunity outside of the island. She had an unconditional love for her mother and would do anything to try to help her recover from the illness. With the help of her brothers, she immediately began gathering all the wood and branches she could find on the island and began to build a boat.

It took Alex and her brothers a total of nine long days and nights to finish building a sturdy boat for the trip. Alex then waited for the sun to rise the next day because she knew that that's when the water was the stillest. Her weak and worried mother kissed her goodbye and gave her a little prayer before sending her on her way.

The journey began very relaxing; therefore, Alex felt comfortable falling asleep for a couple of hours while the boat drifted farther and farther into the sea on its own. Two hours passed, and the water started to become more intense. The waves shook Alex's boat, and she quickly woke up frightened. Before she could do anything about it, a gigantic wave came and crashed upon her. The boat was nearly destroyed, and she was left with nothing but a piece of wood to float on.

She became hopeless and was convinced that her journey had ended there. Then suddenly down the horizon, Alex noticed a huge metal ship sailing her way. She believed it was a miracle! Alex saw this as her only opportunity to be able to survive. Desperately, Alex did everything in her power to wave the ship down and get the passengers' attention. Luckily, one of the sailors saw the young girl struggling and quickly went to rescue her.

A tall, Caucasian man dressed in a white and navy blue suit reached out to Alex and pulled her onto the ship. At first, Alex was frightened because she had never had any affiliations with anyone but the few people who lived on the island, so the experience was very new to her. Trying to comfort Alex, two of the female sailors wrapped a fur blanket around her and prepared her a meal.

Filled with curiosity, the men on the ship interrogated Alex as they tried to understand why she was stranded in the middle of the ocean all on her own. Alex's voice became shaky as she explained to the men that she was searching for medication in order to save her drastically sick mother. She also explained to them that the island she lived in was extremely poor and that the only unlimited amount of resource they had was salt. However, salt was completely useless for them because food was also a scarce resource.

The men's eyes instantly grew wider as they glanced at one another. The young Caucasian man that helped Alex onto the ship quickly jumped up and explained to Alex that the reason they were sailing the seas was because they were in search of some salt. The king back in their country was not pleased with the palace men because the food they prepared for him always lacked flavor. They had all types of spices and herbs at the kingdom, except salt. Therefore, the king demanded these men set voyage over the seas and bring back some salt.

Alex's eyes gleamed with excitement as she initiated a brilliant idea that could help both her and the sailors. She suggested that they make a fair trade: an entire ship loaded with salt, in exchange for food and medication for the island. Without hesitation, the men agreed and instantly made a long journey through the night.

After a long and tiring trip, Alex and the sailors finally made it back safely to the island. Alex immediately ran to her mother excited about telling her the great news, but when she found her, she was in a worse condition than how she was before she had left. Alex's excitement quickly turned into grief.

At that moment, she knew she couldn't waste any more time, so she acted quickly. She called out as many people from the island as she could to quickly help her load the ship with salt. The people, eager to help Alex save her mother's life, worked as fast as they could and were able to finish by nightfall. Aware of the unstable weather conditions, Alex insisted the trip be made and convinced the men to leave that same night.

The trip started out rocky but nothing too serious, until it struck midnight that is. The angry waves were harshly crashing onto the ship shifting it back and forth. The thunder grew louder, and the rain started to fall even harder. For a sudden moment after, everything became extremely quiet and still. Then out of nowhere, BAM! A killer wave crashed onto the ship completely wrecking it. Millions of gallons of salt were spread throughout the entire ocean! And the passengers... lost in the sea forever.

It didn't take long after that for the king to receive the tragic news of the incident. Compassionate about the occurrence, the wealthy king sent out two metal ships loaded with medical supplies, food, water, and clothes. The people from the island were extremely grateful for the king's generous gesture, so they returned the favor by sending him back some more salt.

Unfortunately, Alex did not make it back home, but she was successful at saving her mother's life. Alex's mother became healthy again, and she lived the rest of her life appreciating her daughter's courageous efforts in saving her life.

About the Author

Daisy Sekly is a young motivated college student working to earn a Ph.D. in psychology. Her plan for the future is to become a skillful psychologist working with adolescents. She understands her road to success will not be any easy one, but with God and her loving parents by her side, she is determined to accomplish her greatest dreams.

Passion for Revenge

Alexandria Stapleton

"If you can tell stories, create characters, devise incidents, and have sincerity and passion, it doesn't matter a damn how you write."

Somerset Maugham

Daisy was a young, beautiful eighteen-year-old girl, living in New York City, New York. After graduating as valedictorian from Las Palmas High School in 2001, she was ready to take on what the future held for her. Daisy planned to attend Yale University and study philosophy in the fall. Until one night she experienced something that would change her life forever.

As a young college student things were getting hard financially, emotionally and physically. While taking classes at Yale, Daisy was also working night shifts at a local bar. Daisy had money but no free time in between classes, and her job she was unable to keep up efficiently. She was in need of something to keep her going, so she could be successful in all areas; she turned to cocaine as her boost.

After trying it once, she was hooked and was convinced drugs were the answer to her success. She wasn't able to sleep and that gave her the time to keep up with the homework from all of her classes. Daisy was missing one thing: she needed more drugs.

Professor Looh had been teaching at Yale for thirty years. He had a Ph.D. in Psychology and always kept thirty grams of cocaine in the trunk of his car. The school knew him as a professor, but Daisy knew him as her drug dealer. Daisy would always have an uneasy feeling when she was around him. And not just because they were trading drugs and money, but he would look at her up and down, constantly trying to get close to her.

One night, Daisy and a few of her roommates decided to go out of town for a rave that only came year around. She wasn't feeling like herself after the drinks and the drugs she had consumed, so she stepped outside feeling the cool breeze hit her face. Just then, she saw a girl running towards her and a man chasing after her. The scent of alcohol and cologne hit her suddenly; Daisy fell on the hard, wet ground. She heard a familiar voice say her name.

The voice was loud and raspy, and when she opened her eyes, a dark figure was kneeling over her. The smell of cigarettes and cologne overwhelmed her; her legs were cold and wet. Daisy's whole body was throbbing as she felt the pressure of a man on top of her. Daisy helplessly tried to scream for help, but the man quickly put a knife to her throat. She tried to stay as silent as she could, trapped.

She woke up the next morning in her dorm without any recollection of how she got there. Bruised where no one could see and where only she could feel, Daisy was unsure of the events of the night before and didn't know if it was the drugs or a terrible reality.

The search was on; Daisy was on high alert for the truth about that night and wouldn't stop until she got justice. Going to the police wasn't an option. All they would do is accuse her of being irresponsible while under the influence. She felt ashamed to share her experience with anyone else, so she decided to deal with the problem on her own. She tracked down everyone she remembered seeing that night. She started with her roommates. They told her she disappeared around eleven from the club to go outside, but they didn't see her after that.

Daisy didn't know where she was the rest of the night or who she was with. She remembered the smell of cigarettes and cologne and knew if she came by that smell again, she wouldn't let it pass by.

The next day, she went back to the club where she had been with her friends. She asked if anyone had seen her that night. The bouncer recognized her and said she was getting into a blood red corvette.

The only car she knew like that belonged to Dan Looh.

She arrived at his meeting spot like nothing was wrong and made a deal. She could smell the cigarettes on his breath and the cologne on his shirt. Her heart pounded in her chest as she realized she had found the man that raped her. She was obsessed with the idea that one day he would get what he deserved. Daisy had such passion for her revenge; she was determined to do anything to fulfill what she longed to do.

For weeks, Daisy would sit in her car and watch him as he lived his double life. She followed him around town and continued to make deals. She was overwhelmed with the idea of her revenge and would stop at nothing to get it right. She wasn't eating or sleeping properly; she was high on cocaine and refused to come down. After weeks of passionately plotting, Daisy had come up with the perfect revenge. It would look like an accident.

On February 14, 2002, Daisy was not celebrating Valentine's Day. She was celebrating the death of Dan Looh. That morning, before the sun came up, she tiptoed through his house, pouring gasoline all over the place. The couch, the kitchen floor and the

174

bedrooms were covered. She walked into his bedroom and watched as he slept peacefully, and she wondered how he could live himself after what he had done to her.

Daisy wouldn't let it happen again, so she took out her lighter and dropped it beside him. She watched as he went up in flames. She felt chills overcome her body. She felt as if she was in control of everything. Daisy felt complete. Before he could blink, he and his house were gone. Dan Looh had gotten what he deserved; Daisy ran out of the house and never looked back. Police were unable to find who caused the fire but later found out about the professor's other hobbies and closed the case.

Five years later, Daisy graduated from Yale University with a Ph.D. in psychology and was ready to start her career as therapist for rape and assault victims. She was five years sober.

Unfortunately, on February 14, 2007, she was found unresponsive in her apartment with third degree burns from an accidental fire. Daisy died on her way to the hospital. The autopsy of Daisy later confirmed that the cause of her death wasn t the fire but a fatal drug overdose. Daisy's death was no accident but a little something called karma.

About the Author

Alexandria Stapleton is an outgoing, spunky nineteen year old. She lives in a small town and is finishing her first year at Crafton Hills College. She plans to transfer to a Cal State and graduate with a Bachelor's degree. She has not decided what career she wants to take on yet, but she is very open minded and trusts she will find the perfect one for herself! She is young and has her whole life ahead of her.

The story she wrote caused her to really think about what she can accomplish and what she can do with a few crazy scenarios.

Meeting My Other Half

Haylee Vaughan

You give me that bottom of the ninth,

last at bat, tied game, grand slam,

full of butterflies kinda feeling!

Haylee Vaughan

About six months ago, in July of 2015, Haylee's life changed for the better. She was sitting on her bed one Sunday night when she got a message on Okcupid, an online dating website, from a man named Kyle. The message caught her eye, so she looked at the man's profile and saw many things she liked.

First, she thought he was handsome with his blonde/brownish hair and blue/grey eyes. But what really made her want to message him back was not his looks but the things about him. He said in his profile that he was a family man, coached baseball, had a steady job, and was outgoing and down to earth.

After reading a little bit about him, she messaged him back. After a few short messages back and forth, she gave Kyle her number. He immediately texted her saying, "Hi, Haylee. It's Kyle." Haylee was lying on her bed, and her phone went off and she saw the message and got the biggest grin on her face and texted him back. They texted all night while he was at work doing inventory. Monday came around, and they texted each other all day long.

On Tuesday night, as Haylee was sitting on the couch watching TV with her mom, she was texting Kyle as she had been since Sunday night. As they

181

were texting trying to get to know each other better, Kyle told her he used to work at Stater Brothers. As soon as Haylee read that message, she put her hand on her head and said, "Oh, crap! What family members does he know?" Half her family worked for Stater Brothers. Haylee asked him, "What is the store number you worked at?" He replied with, "Store number 001. Why?" Haylee looked at her mom and asked her, "Have you worked at this store?" Her mom said, "Yeah a long time ago, but he may know your aunt Michelle."

So, Haylee asked Kyle, "Do you know a Michelle Lerma?" He was said, "Yeah. I am good friends with her daughters. I haven't seen her in a long time. How do you know her?" Haylee freaked out and was saying to her mom, "Oh, my gosh! He knows Michelle. How is this possible? This is crazy." She texted him back and said, "Ummm… that is my aunt." He said, "No way! You are kidding me right?" She said, "No, that is my aunt." He said, "So, you must know the Hemmerlings then?" Haylee said, "Yes, they are family friends." Kyle said, "I used to coach their son Nathan's travel ball team." Haylee was freaking that Kyle knew some of her family already.

After that, Haylee immediately texted her cousin Jenn to see if she really did know him and she did. Later that night at about 8pm, Kyle asked if he could call Haylee and tell her good night. She was nervously lying on her floor waiting for him to call her. When he did, she answered thinking the phone call would be about ten minutes or so. They started talking about how he knows her family and how they both were at Jenn's baby shower but had never even seen each other.

They ended up in a deep conversation about their families, how Kyle is the oldest of nine and has twenty-three cousins. Also, they discussed how Haylee is the youngest of five and has fourteen nieces and nephews. As Haylee was lying on the floor charging her phone and talking to that man, time went on and on and on. Haylee kept telling Kyle, "You need to go to bed; you have to work in the morning." Kyle would not listen to her and eventually, it was time for Kyle to go to work. By the time he got to work and they hung up the phone, it had been seven hours. During that phone call, Kyle and Haylee decided to meet each other the next day.

On Wednesday morning, Haylee texted Kyle, "Good morning." Haylee had to work that morning, so she got up and got ready for work. The whole time she was texting Kyle, she could not stop smiling. Haylee went to work at BJ's Brewhouse still with the biggest smile on her face. When she got to work, everyone there kept asking her, "Why are you so happy today?" All Haylee could do was smile and say, "I met this amazing guy." After Haylee got off work, she had to go home and get ready for practice. Haylee coached her nieces' softball team in Fontana. She headed to practice with the guy on her mind.

Once she got to practice, she was trying to focus and coach the little girls, but her mind was not there. She was on cloud nine thinking about the guy and how amazing he was. She was so excited but nervous to meet him that night. When practice was over, she hurried home to get ready. She had to shower and make sure she smelled good and looked pretty for the new guy.

She headed to the baseball park he was coaching at. His All-Star team had a game that night. As Haylee got to the field, she saw two parking lots and did not know which one to park in, so she circled and circled until she found a spot in one of the parking lots. Once she found a spot, she looked down at the fields and got freaked out because there were a lot of people at the field. She decided to stay in her car until the game was over because she was too scared to go down there. As she sat in the car feeling scared, she texted her cousin Jenn. Haylee asked Jenn what she thought about Kyle. Jenn said he was a great guy and that Haylee should go for it.

After the game was over, Kyle called Haylee to see where she was. Haylee told him she was in the parking lot to the left side of the field. Kyle told her to come over to the parking lot on the right side because that was where he was parked. Haylee drove over to the other parking lot with her heart in her throat and butterflies in her stomach. After she parked, she got out of the car to finally meet the amazing man she had been talking to and texting for the last several days. After they said hi, they walked over to Kyle's truck and sat on the tailgate and talked. He was telling her about the game and how it went.

At one point, as they were talking, someone driving by threw a firecracker at the playground next to them. Haylee got so scared that she jumped almost onto Kyle's lap. He just laughed and held her to protect her. They both laughed and said, "There are sparks between us, literality."

After that, Haylee said she had to go, so Kyle walked her back to her car. They were standing next to Haylee's car saying bye when Kyle gave Haylee a hug and leaned in and kissed her. Haylee's heart jumped out of her chest. She was so happy he kissed her. They said their goodbyes and went on their way. Ever since that day that Haylee met Kyle, she has been the happiest girl in a very long time.

About the Author

Haylee Vaughan is twenty-one years old and the youngest of five. She has four older brothers and fourteen nieces and nephews that she would give her life for. She is a true family person. Her family consists of people that could never be replaced and will forever be by her side. She is currently going to school to study to be a kindergarten teacher, as well as holding down a job. One thing that will forever be with her is being young at heart. She loves to go to Disneyland and stay young.

Growing up, she was always around sports and even played herself. She played softball from five years old to seventeen years old. When she thought her life did not have sports anymore, she met a man whose life revolves around sports. That's when she knew for as long as she lives she will be around sports.

Interlaced

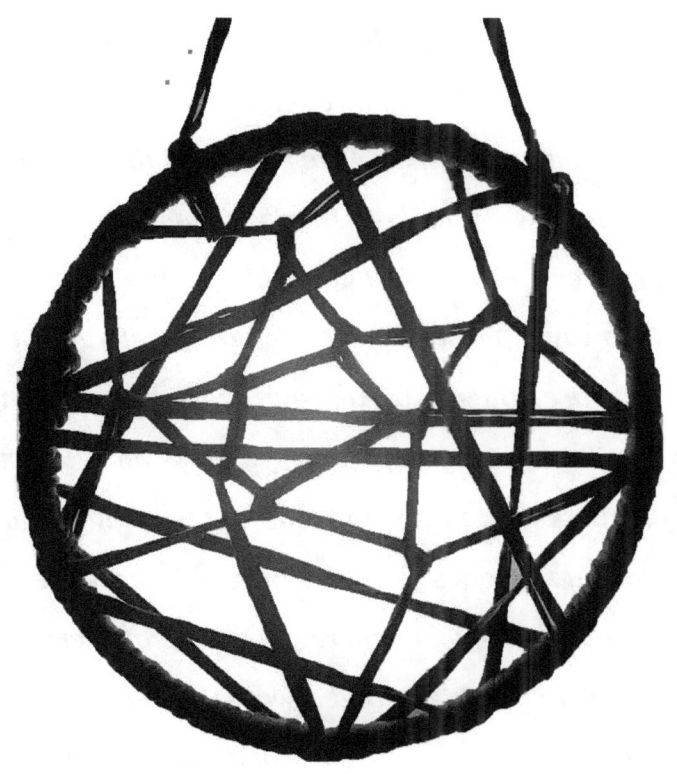

Jessica Yslas

"This life is what you make it. No matter what, you're going to mess up sometimes, it's a universal truth. But the good part is you get to decide how you're going to mess it up. Girls will be your friends - they'll act like it anyway. But just remember, some come, some go. The ones that stay with you through everything - they're your true best friends. Don't let go of them. Also remember, sisters make the best friends in the world. As for lovers, well, they'll come and go too. And baby, I hate to say it, most of them - actually pretty much all of them are going to break your heart, but you can't give up because if you give up, you'll never find your soulmate. You'll never find that half who makes you whole and that goes for everything. Just because you fail once, doesn't mean you're gonna fail at everything.

Keep trying, hold on, and always, always, always believe in yourself, because if you don't, then who will, sweetie? So keep your head high, keep your chin up, and most importantly, keep smiling, because life's a beautiful thing and there's so much to smile about."

Marilyn Monroe

I felt the warmth radiating from his lips that traced the side of my neck. His hands intertwined with mine gave me the feeling of bliss. Sparks flew as our lips met. My hands left his to interlace my hands into his hair. His short black locks smoothly laced around my fingers in an instant. The smell of his skin surrounded me like incense of the woods during the summer. That is the smell that only comes from being in the sun for many hours on end. The muscles pressed against my stomach sent chills down my back. His muscular legs pressed against my legs and mine against his was very exhilarating, and I almost blacked out. He grabbed my hips and rubbed his long and erect partner against my inner thigh.

Then sinking lower, he placed butterfly kisses along my neck. When he reached my breasts, he gathered my right one in his mouth and sucked it. As he eased off it, he flicked his tongue over the nipple. I moaned out of pleasure. As he moved to my left breast, I did not notice his hand slip lower until he touched my mound. He slipped one finger inside of me while sucking on my breast. He started to pulse it in and out. Then, he added another finger. At that moment, he bit the nipple. Slowly, his head slipped lower until his head was between my legs. I could not look at him.

Then, out of nowhere, he said, "Look at me savor you." My eyes shot open as he licked my bud and nibbled on it. My hand intertwined with his hair as he drove his tongue in and out in a pattern. Then, he pulled his tongue out and whispered, "Just like honey." Slowly, he crept up and placed his partner at the entrance of my flower and slowly proceeded to enter.

As he reached my hymen, he stopped and placed his head next to mine and whispered, "This will only hurt a little bit." All I could do was nod my head yes. He quickly pulled back out a little then quickly slammed right back in. I screamed out in pain; then, just as fast as it happened, it dissipated as he held still within me. As soon as I relaxed, he slowly started to move. Then, he started to get faster as I moaned out in joy. He slowly pulled out and laid next to me and whispered, "I love you, Aphrodite."

He gathered me in his arms. As he did, we lay together. He placed his hands on mine. The touch of his strong gentle hands caressing my hips up and down sent chills through my body. He then turned me to face him as he pressed his lips against mine. It gave my heart a little leap of joy. I was ready for more, and so was he.

Damn, his skin sent shock waves of ecstasy through my body. His lips neared my ear as he whispered, "You will always be mine and nobody else's. I will always fight for you even if it costs me my life. Don't you ever forget that my love." He slightly nibbled on my ear as I jolted out of bliss and pulled him closer into my arms. The muscles on his back moved when I touched his upper back; he shivered from my touch.

He whispered in my ear quite sexily, "Only you can make me feel this way. No one else has the power to do this. You should know that I only long for your touch and any one that gets in the way might get hurt." I quickly pulled him closer and whispered in his ear, "I never will forget that but understand that I won't let anyone get as close to you as I am." A smile spread across his face giving my heart a bit of excitement and causing my body to want to touch his more than ever before. I felt so connected to him in every way that my body had always yearned for a feeling, for that emotion.

As my mind blurred from the touch of him, I heard a siren in the background and pleaded it to end. Though the sound only got louder as it got closer, and in shock when the sound was at my ear, I was out of bed in an instant.

I realized that it was the same dream that I have every night with the man I did not know. It has always been the same dream for three years now. I have grown accustomed to seeing him in my dreams. His plush lips, caramel skin, with black hair, with those sky blue eyes that capture my heart as I look at him. Dreams never do come true, or so I thought. Oh, and my name is Aphrodite Adonia.

This was how every day started out for me, so I had decided it was time to do what I normally did in the morning. I got up and walked to my bathroom to look at myself in the mirror and decided it was time to get ready. I turned on the water and splashed my face clearing my mind of any doubts that I had about myself. I slipped out of my silky pajamas and walked to the shower to turn it on. As I did so, it occurred to me that my parents did not to bother to wake me up yet again. So that meant either I was up before them or I was late, but the time on my clock showed that I was up long before them.

So, I decided to take it slow and steady. I washed my hair with my pomegranate shampoo and conditioned it with my coconut conditioner. The reason why I chose those two smells was they blended together to create his smell. I did it so if I was sad at school or something, I could smell my hair and think of him. I know it sounds weird and all, but it relaxes me when I get even the slightest scent of him.

Later, after a long walk to school and three gruesome class periods, I ended up in my favorite class, chemistry, and in that class was my best friend Kim Eira. That day, we got to work in groups for the lab though labs are usually worked in groups of three. We only had two since our other member went to a continuation school because he was so far behind. The labs seemed to be taking longer than they usually did for us to finish them though we finished the lab before anyone else in class.

So, Kim and I decided to talk though every time we did, she would always ask about my dreams. Even though she would ask, I would turn the conversation back to her and ask her what her dream had been that night. In the middle of our conversation, our sensei came in with a new student and asked everyone to stop what they were doing, so he could introduce him to the entire class.

I did not look up until he said the new kid's name, which happened to be Dmitri Knight. When I did look up, my jaw dropped. Just the thought of saying his name felt as if it would just roll off my lips. In the middle of my thoughts, my gaze traveled from his luscious lips to his memorizing eyes. That is when both of our eyes widened though his not as much as mine. To my side, I heard my friend whisper in my ear, "Wow! What is wrong with you? You look as if you've seen a ghost or are you just into him, because I can see why. He is so damn fine."

Out of the corner of my eye, I saw my friend with the biggest grin I had ever seen her have before. I looked back to the front to be gazed upon by eyes that were making my heart melt in an instant. In my defense, it was because I was staring into the eyes of the man I had dreamed of for three years. I was so entranced that I did not even hear sensei call me.

As I came back into reality, I heard the sensei say, "Aphrodite, did you hear me?" All I could say was, "I'm sorry, sir. I did not hear you. Could you repeat it, please?" Doctor Nelson sadly shook his head and said, "Well, Aphrodite, maybe you should listen more often, so that I would not have to repeat things, but you know what I will repeat this only one time, so you are sure to listen to what I say. Do you understand me, Aphrodite?" All I said was, "Yes, sir. I do."

Dr. Nelson then repeated what he had said earlier, "Aphrodite, you will be showing Dmitri around school and to his classes since most of your classes are the same. Now that we have that settled, Dmitri please go take that empty seat next to her and get out some paper and a pen or pencil." As Dmitri walked towards me, we never lost eye contact. As he came to our seats, he literally sat next to me. In our school, we have the desks that are meant to be two separate desks, but they were selected to stay as one desk in order to save money for the school district and to save room in the classrooms.

As he sat down on his side of the desk, our hands touched slightly as he sat down beside me. As we touched, a shock shot through my body making it so I was even more alert of him next to me.

I could tell that he saw me jump slightly though he did not say a thing for the rest of the period; also, he tried not to even touch me at all, even if it was a slight tap or brush of the arms. For the next few minutes, I zoned out as I did my work. However, I was cautious of my surrounding, especially since the man I had dreamed of was sitting next to me. As soon as the bell rang, my best friend Kim turned to the both of us and said, "Hey, let's go get lunch. I'm starving."

I looked over at Dmitri Knight and smiled at him while asking, "Would you be all right with that? And, if you want I'll show you around after we eat." He smiled and man did that smile melt my heart when it came upon his face and he said, "Sure, I'd love that."

As we packed up our bags, Kim complained that we were taking too long by saying, "Hurry up. I'm wasting away here. Look, I'm gonna just be skin and bones real soon." As we got up from our sets, our arms brushed against each other sending a shock wave of heat rushing through my whole body. We both jumped back from each other's touch. I looked and saw by the look on his face that he had felt it as well. As we neared the cafeteria, I asked him if he wanted to come with me to get lunch, not knowing if he had his lunch with him. He said, "Why not? I am kind of hungry."

As we walked towards the lunch line, I put my focus on the floor in front of me. As we entered the cafeteria, every girl in line began to glare at me for being next to him. All of a sudden, I was pushed from behind and started to fall into Dmitri's chest. All he could do was stare in shock at what happened, as he held me in his arms.

"Wow... are you alright?" asked Dmitri.

"Um...yea, but can I ask you something?" I asked.

"Sure, what is it?" responded Dmitri.

Shyly, I asked loud enough so only he could hear what I was going to say, "Can you get your hand off my boob? It is really uncomfortable."

"Oh, my God! I am so sorry. I did not realize I was doing that. I am so sorry!" Panicked, Dmitri quickly removed his hand and put it in his pocket.

Once Dmitri's hand was off my breast, we started to walk again.

At that time, in Dmitri's mind all he could think was, *Holy shipwreck. Her breasts are perfect. They felt so good. I felt as if I were in heaven. They were the perfect size; they fit so nicely in my hands. Oh, shit! Why did I have to walk behind her? Her ass is perfect. I just want to grab her like I do in those dreams and just blow her mind. Crap! I can't think this way or else I will not be able to control myself.*

As Dmitri and I got closer to the check-out stand with our lunch, I felt something rub up against me from behind, but I did not have the guts to turn around to see what it was. As we exited the cafeteria, girls kept staring at us both. Then out of nowhere, Dmitri leaned down to my ear and whispered, "I am sorry, but if you want them to stop staring then I will leave, if that is what you want."

I turned towards him and said, "What? No, don't do that! You would be stampeded by a bunch of girls if I left you alone." His eyes were wide as he stared at me due to my response. We continued on down towards Kim, when all of a sudden Dmitri pulled me into an empty hall and shoved me against a wall. I was stunned by his sudden action. I did not know what to do.

"Look at me, Aphrodite..." was all Dmitri said to me. "I know that you know me and from where we know each other. So, tell me was everything in the dreams real for you as it was for me or was it all a lie?" Before I could even respond his lips collided with my own, which silenced me in a split second. His lips were breathtaking, as we held each other in a desperate attempt to solidify our unspoken feelings for one another. My arms circled around his neck in order to gain better access to his mouth. I pulled his head closer as my tongue swiped across his lips asking for permission to enter. He quickly opened his mouth, which let our tongues collide with one another's.

That was the first time I had done that to him. Usually, he was the one to ask entrance- well, at least in our dreams. As we struggled to dominate each other, his hand dipped down to my hips, which shocked me because we were still at school, and I was worried that we would be caught. I slightly pushed against his chest, which caused him to break our kiss. He stared at me with a perplexed face; he was probably wondering why I had done that when it was just getting good.

"Stop, we can't do this here. We will get caught, and we won't be able to see each other for a long time..." I stated that while looking into his chest, because I was afraid that if I had been looking into his eye, we would have just continued from where we had left, before I pushed him away.

"So, we can continue this later when we are alone?" asked Dmitri.

"Yes, we can. Now, let's get back to Kim before she comes looking for us," I stated.

"Too late! I already found you two. So, when were you going to tell me that you two knew each other?" stated Kim, as she stood with her hand on her hips looking very upset with me for not saying anything to her. Stunned, I stood speechless for a few moments, until I felt a hand placed on my hip while pulling me back into Dmitri's chest.

A smile crept onto Kim's mouth as she stated, "So, is this the guy from the dream you told me about? If not, then I am going to be furious with you!"

"Yes, it is him, so please don't say anything to anyone." I replied as a blush crept onto my face. As I said that, I felt a squeeze on my hip and a bump on my lower back.

"Why would I tell anyone? From what you have told me about this dream it means you are meant to be together or at least that is what I think." She smiled as she told us this. "Now come on. You two can make out once you two go home, or wherever you two decide to go after school today. Right now, I am hungry, so let's go eat."

We all laughed as we walked to Kim's and my favorite place to eat lunch. Nobody knew about it except us two ... and well now, Dmitri of course. As we walked Dmitri's hand never left my hip.

After school, Dmitri and I walked to my house slowly, while talking about different subjects. We looked like a normal pair of kids that were best friends, but the on looker would never know unless they were one of us what we really were to each other.

When we reached my house, I opened the door and yelled, "Mom, I'm home, and I have a friend with me!" Thumps were heard as my mother came running from upstairs towards us wanting to know who I brought by. When she saw Dmitri, she stopped in her tracks and stood there with her mouth open.

My mother slowly walked towards Dmitri and me as she mumbled, "How? I thought your father was with Samantha back in Britain? What are you doing here? Why did they not contact me...your parents knew of the agreement ... you guys weren't supposed to meet for another five years. What is going on?" All of a sudden my house phone went off. Nervously, I reached for the phone and answered it saying, "Adonia residence. You are speaking with Aphrodite. How can I help you?"

"Um...Yes, can I speak to your mother, sweetie?" said the soft female voice on the other end of the telephone line. For some odd reason, she sounded nervous.

"Sure, one moment....Mom, the phone is for you," I stated as she flung her hand out for the phone.

"Why didn't you tell me you were coming back?" my mother spit out at the phone in anger. "Yea, well guess what...? Now they have to know because they are both here in my living room together! Get you round white ass over here right now, or else I will drag you over here!" My mother yelled as she pressed 'end' on the phone.

Fifteen minutes later, the doorbell rang, and my mother flung the door open so hard that the windows shook in the whole house. My mother was furious, or so I thought. As Dmitri and I looked towards the front entrance of the house, my mother was enveloping a woman with dark brown hair and blue eyes in a tight hug, and they were both crying as they held each other.

The other woman pulled back and said, "Sorry for not keeping in contact these past few years. Do you forgive me?"

"Of course, Sammy. I will always forgive you for anything you do or don't do!" My weeping mother stated. Dmitri slowly walked forward and said, "Mom, what is going on?"

"Oh, honey. I need you and Aphrodite to sit down. It is a long story, and well... never mind, we are going to sum it up really quick for you two... Well, you two are actually supposed to..." She was cut off before she could finish what she was going to say to us as a man barged in saying, "Love, don't tell them anything. We must let them get to know each other, and on their own, we must let their love blossom."

Without even trying, I knew what to say. "Mom, you don't have to worry. We already know because, we have been in contact for the past three years." As I looked around the room, I saw all the parents' mouths wide open in shock.

"WHAT!!!!!!!" shouted all our parents in unison; it was so loud that I thought that my ear drums would break. Then, Dmitri's hand intertwined with my own as we stood before them, and he let me tell how we sort of already knew about what was going on between our families. Okay, so we lied... Oh, well. I guessed we would find out soon or later. I hoped for sooner.

As we stood with our backs to the wall, I saw Dmitri look at me from the corner of his eye as our parents discussed what we had told them. I feared that they would separate us, and as if Dmitri was reading my mind, he squeezed my hand, as if trying to let me know that he was there for me even if everything went south from there on out.

Only the future would tell what was in store for us, and I didn't mind waiting as long as he was next to me, so we could face it together. This was most definitely going to be the hardest journey I would take in my life- that was just based off the look on all of our parents' faces.

Aphrodite and Dmitri will be back for a second time where they will learn what is to become of them and their love. Is it forbidden or is it what they hope it can and will be?

About the Author

Jessica Yslas was born in 1995 and raised in California her entire life. She is the youngest daughter of three and happens to be middle child of five. At the age of twenty, she is currently enrolled in college as an English major in Creative Writing. She intends to become a college professor where she will be able to help people to let their creativity out. Jessica has stated that people should go for their goals even if they think it is impossible, unless it is illegal. In that case, she says, "Don't risk it because that goal would be nothing if you got hurt or sent to jail." This is the first book she has ever been published in and can't wait to have her next book out for the public to read.

About the Editor

Dr. Cassundra White-Elliott resides in California with her family, where as an English/Education professor she teaches at various community colleges and universities.

When writing, she writes with the direction of the Holy Spirit, in an effort to share with God's people all that He has for them.

In addition to teaching and writing, Dr. White-Elliott also serves as an evangelistic teacher. She is also the founder of International Women's Commission, a ministry that serves the needs of the entire person, by attending to healing the mind, body, soul, and spirit.

Dr. White-Elliott holds a Ph.D. in Education, a Master's in English Composition, and a Bachelor's in Education.

Dr. White-Elliott is also the founder of CLF Publishing, LLC. For your publishing needs, go online to www.clfpublishing.org.

Get your copy of the first "Mosaic" at barnesandnoble.com or amazon.com.

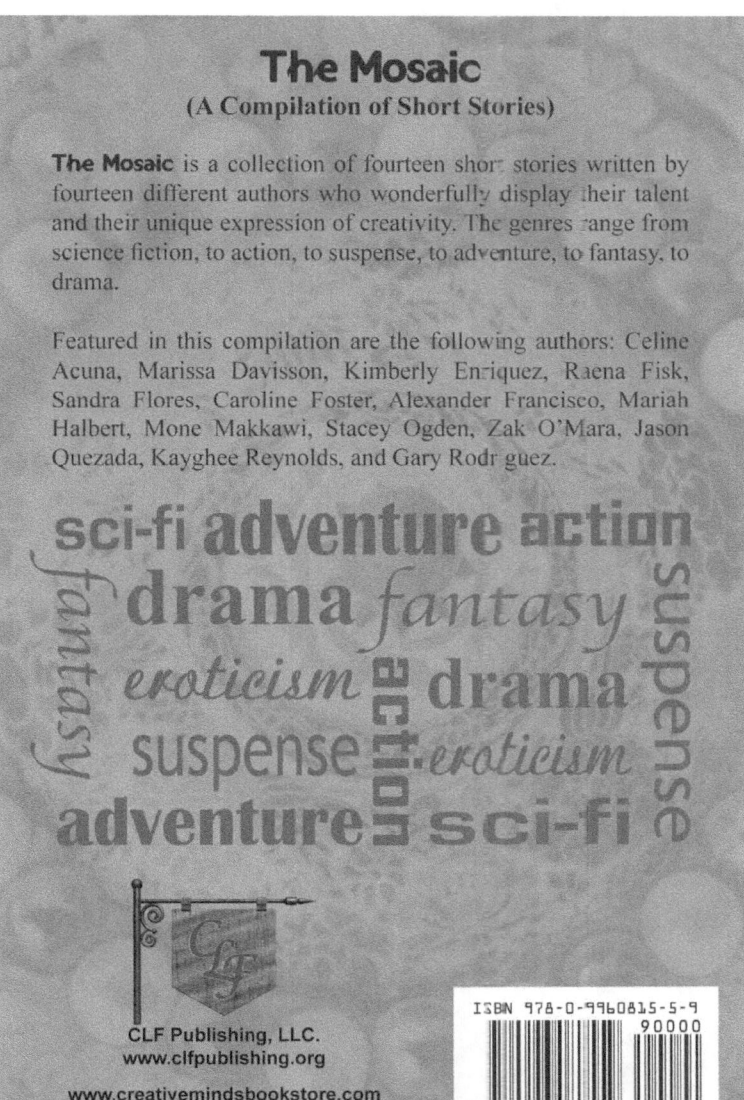

The Mosaic
(A Compilation of Short Stories)

The Mosaic is a collection of fourteen short stories written by fourteen different authors who wonderfully display their talent and their unique expression of creativity. The genres range from science fiction, to action, to suspense, to adventure, to fantasy, to drama.

Featured in this compilation are the following authors: Celine Acuna, Marissa Davisson, Kimberly Enriquez, Raena Fisk, Sandra Flores, Caroline Foster, Alexander Francisco, Mariah Halbert, Mone Makkawi, Stacey Ogden, Zak O'Mara, Jason Quezada, Kayghee Reynolds, and Gary Rodriguez.

sci-fi adventure action
fantasy drama *fantasy* suspense
eroticism action drama suspense
suspense action *eroticism*
adventure action sci-fi

CLF Publishing, LLC.
www.clfpublishing.org

www.creativemindsbookstore.com
www.amazon.com
www.barnesandnoble.com

ISBN 978-0-9960815-5-9
90000

9 730996 081559

It is a wonderful collection of short stories from a variety of genres.